DRAGON THIEF SERIES

SEASON ONE
Dragon Thief
The Chicago Job
The Poisons Book Job
The Vault Job
The Femme Fatale Job
The Scavenger Job

SEASON TWO
The Crown of Kingship Job
The Green Scroll Job
The Payback Job

THE FEMME FATALE JOB

A Dragon Thief story

Dragon Thief
Book Five

Kat Simons

T&D PUBLISHING

THE FEMME FATALE JOB

For my family, always...

ONE

Myra strolled under the canopy of trees, the bright winter sun filtering down through evergreen branches along the paved path through the middle of Central Park. The Bethesda Fountain was ahead of her, Strawberry Fields behind her, and most of the tourists clumped up in those places so that her stroll was pleasantly people free. The lake to her left peeked out around raised black rocks and greenery, but she didn't take the diverted path to watch the paddle boats. Though it was the middle of winter, the air crisp and frosty at the moment, the lake hadn't frozen, and there were just enough tourists willing to take out a paddle boat even in the cold to keep the service open a little longer.

The Boathouse restaurant wasn't far away, but

she wasn't heading there either. She was ambling. Enjoying the day. No where specific to be.

Waiting for him to find her.

It didn't take him long. He never took very long finding her. In fact, he had an uncanny ability to find her even when she hadn't given him a place to look.

He fell into step beside her, a very tall presence, standing easily a head or more over everyone else around them. He had a good foot and a half on her, which might have been awkward, but she had a real soft spot for tall men.

She had an even softer spot for Christopher.

She glanced at him from the corner of her eye. He was wearing a shirt. A button up business shirt in a soft pink color under a long tan coat. And instead of the dress slacks he normally wore, he was wearing jeans. It was a strange sort of combination, nothing she'd seen him in before. She'd mostly seen him in his flight outfit—pants, no shoes, no shirt so he could shift enough to release his wings. The fact that he was wearing a coat, which she didn't think he needed, and shoes, which he didn't like to wear, made it obvious he was attempting to appear human. Or at the very least, blend in with the humans so he didn't draw too much attention.

Given that he was nearly seven foot tall, it was

impossible for him not to draw attention. But it was always possible the tourists assumed he was a basketball player. This was New York after all. Lots of people could be found walking the paths through the Park.

She bumped his arm with her shoulder, using the excuse of getting that close to him to breathe in his uniquely Christopher scent, that mix of dragon shifter—heat and musk and a very faint hint of brimstone—and some sort of soap that she associated purely with him. No sugar cookie scent at that moment, but she liked when he smelled like this soap of his, too.

"You look good in business casual wear."

"Thank you," he said, his voice deep and rumbling. He tilted his head slightly toward her. "I'm not sure the camouflage is working as well as I'd like."

"It would help if you weren't as tall as some of the trees."

"I can't be sorry for that," he said. "Because you like tall men."

She huffed, tried to swallow her pleased laugh. "I do."

She let her gaze move over the path, skim the scattering of people walking around them. Christopher was drawing stares, but most people looked away quickly. She couldn't tell if they recognized him or not. There weren't any pictures of the royal family allowed in magazines and newspapers. But he did occasionally show up at events with his father, and sometimes in gossip columns. Or at least, he had shown up in the gossip columns at one stage, by name, but he hadn't been in them recently.

Even if people didn't recognize him as the dragon king's son, though, they might still recognize him as a dragon shifter. A lot of the dragon shifters were hard to miss, even in human form.

Not that she'd known that much about them before meeting Christopher. She'd gone out of her way to avoid all things dragon. She mostly stuck to robbing humans, and rich humans at that. Like her soft spot for tall men, she also had a soft spot for stealing from people who already had more than they could keep track of and often didn't even notice when some of their stuff went missing. There was something very satisfying about taking a valuable object from someone like that. And then making herself a small fortune in the process.

Keeping under the radar so she could do her job, though, meant staying under the radar of the movers and shakers in the city. The powerful people.

The dragon king.

She'd blown that up by taking an ill-considered bet and breaking into the king's hoard. A challenge she hadn't been able to resist. The hoard was supposed to be impossible to break into. And if she hadn't been caught standing in the middle of all that wealth, perusing all the fine objects and valuables, looking for something tiny and relatively worthless to take to prove she'd been in the hoard, she wouldn't have ever gotten tangled up with dragon shifters. She would have happily continued to avoid them and everything about them.

But then the king had sent her to rescue his "youngling." That youngling turned out to be a fully grown man. Who was distractingly tall. And strangely attractive in a way that couldn't be described as handsome.

And her life hadn't been the same since.

She regretted getting caught breaking into the king's hoard. She didn't like at all having the dragon king think she worked for him now, or that she was somehow beholden to him. She hated that the dragon king thought of her as one of *his* people.

She did *not* hate that she'd met Christopher.

Unfortunately, his father was a problem. One they needed to deal with before the undefined and very new thing between them went any farther than the few kisses they'd shared and the two technical dates they'd been on. One watching a movie on a screen he'd set up on the balcony of one of his apartments. The second, just a few nights ago, when they'd sat on that same balcony watching the sun rise.

She wrapped her black wool coat around her a little tighter, not because she was cold but because she needed something to do with her hands so she wouldn't automatically reach for his.

"Let's go disappear into the Ramble," she said. "Easier to talk without you drawing all this attention."

He nodded, his own hands stuffed into his pockets as they strolled at a measured pace to a section of forest that spread across the middle the Park. Winding dirt paths twisted through thick, dense woodlands, though the oak and maple limbs were bare now, giving the area a lovely stark effect. Dark rocky outcroppings rose up around corners in the bending paths, and sun flittered down to the fern and vine underbrush.

They followed the paths, encountering a handful of birders as they moved deeper into the woods. The feeling of being in a city disappeared. Even the smell was all nature, dirt and trees, dried leaves and pine. Myra could almost believe they were walking through the woods in Upstate New York, far away from everything they had to deal with.

When she was certain they were alone, with no random people around the next bend, she broached the reason for this meeting. "What did your father say?"

Christopher's mouth tightened. "Not as much as I wanted. He refused to acknowledge what he told you about having plans for me. He won't admit to any such thing. He's a stubborn old bastard." This last said under his breath, with a twist of annoyance to his mouth.

"Did he tell you I lied about what he'd said?" She was more curious than offended. The king was used to manipulations and lies. She wouldn't put it past him. Especially since he'd made it clear he disapproved of her relationship with Christopher, even as he kept attempting to make her one of his "humans," one of the humans known to work for him.

"He didn't, actually. He claimed you misremembered."

"Huh. I would have expected him to just say I lied."

"I found the hedge interesting, too. He likes you."

"No, he doesn't. He set me up to be killed."

The last job the king had hired her for had put her in the way of a wizard who'd tried to shoot her. Twice. That wasn't usually something a person who liked you did.

"*Like* is maybe a strong word. Admire. He admires you. And I was right. That job was a test. A test he claims he thought you'd pass."

"If I survived, I'm worthy, right?" She snorted, a sardonic sound of her own.

She didn't want the king's admiration or to be worthy in his attention. She didn't give two fucks about whether he found her worthy or not. She just wanted him to leave her alone now.

"That fits with his way of thinking," Christopher said on a sigh.

"And when you told him I'm not working for him again?"

Christopher let out a hissing sort of growl. A sound she associated with dragon shifters. A sound no human made. "He smiled," Christopher said. "He claimed you'd change your mind."

"Wow. He's never been so wrong about anything before. I do not intend on changing my mind."

"I know." Christopher's shoulders hunched as he scowled down at the dirt path, his hands still firmly in his coat pockets. "He mentioned something…"

"Another job?" She narrowed her eyes at him.

"Not…technically. But, it's a situation that…" He trailed off and looked out at the trees, turning his face away from her.

But not before she saw the color rise in his cheeks, the red blush coloring his high, sharp cheekbones.

He was blushing. That could only mean one thing.

"There's a damsel in distress, isn't there?"

She pressed her lips together so she wouldn't grin. He was sensitive about this particular soft spot of his. Her attempt not to smile failed miserably, though, so she just gave in. She loved that he was a dragon with a soft spot for damsels in distress. In fact, it was one of the things about him she liked the most.

But the character trait got him razzed by the other dragons. The trait had also been exploited by the people who'd kidnapped him.

"There might be," he mumbled.

"You know he's manipulating you, right? To get you to do what he wants you to."

"Yes." Still a mumble.

"But you'd like my help saving this damsel anyway because this is a damsel in distress situation?"

"Yes." He admitted with a sigh.

She bumped his arm again. "For you, I'll help. But not for the king. For you."

Without looking at her, he took one hand out of his pocket and stretched it out to her. She only hesitated a beat before taking hold of his hand and twinning her fingers with his. His hand was so much bigger than hers, he completely engulfed her. But he was also exceptionally gentle with that size and strength. She never worried about him hurting her.

He squeezed gently and she felt his muscles relaxing as they walked.

"My father *claims* he will no longer attempt to hire you," Christopher said. "He *says* he understands you prefer your independence and do not want to accept the protection of the dragons."

"Protection?" She snorted. The king had a funny idea of the word "protection" if he thought sending her on a job to get killed qualified.

"He hasn't given up on trying to pull you into his permanent employ," Christopher said. "He'll likely keep trying. But for now, he's pretending to let you go your own way."

"I see." She did. It was a game for the king. But…

Where did that leave her and Christopher?

Two

They reached a rocky outcropping just off a path, the black collection of stone forming natural seat shapes as it rose above the dried leaves and dirt of the thickly wooded Ramble. Without a word, they both settled on the rocks, close enough Myra could feel Christopher's body heat along one side of her body, a warm contrast to the cold stone under her. In the distance, she could hear the bubbling sounds of the manmade stream running through the Ramble and quiet bird twittering overhead. Good day for the birders.

She turned to face Christopher, pulling one leg up onto the rock and wrapping her arms around her knee. "Tell me about this damsel and her current distress."

Christopher pulled in a deep breath. She ignored the way that made his shoulders and chest expand to stretch the fabric of his tan coat tight. For a moment she worried he'd tear through the thick wool.

"Her name is Issa and she works for a couple of plastic surgeons on the Upper East Side. Receptionist, not a nurse, but she's currently in school to get a degree in medical billing so she can move jobs."

Myra rested her chin on her raised knee, watching Christopher's expression closely as he spoke. Tension around his jaw, faint lines around his narrowed eyes. Yeah, definitely a distressed Issa had him unhappy.

"Is she human?" She could be a shifter. She could be a wizard. She could be a human with other magical skills that didn't fall into wizardcraft, like Myra's own touch of thief's magic. Or Issa could be one of the millions of ordinary humans just trying to get through the day.

What she wasn't likely to be was a dragon shifter.

Because Myra had known so little about dragon shifters before meeting Christopher, she hadn't realized there were so few female dragons in the world, that they were so fundamentally scary and violent, that they lived a hell of a lot longer than the males, and that they were, most of them, currently sound asleep. Like the few real dragons that existed in the world. Something to do with living for millennia encouraged centuries-long naps, apparently.

Among the ordinary—if that word even applied—dragon shifters walking around not sleeping, there were apparently a number of nonbinary individuals, and a lot of males. But at the moment, few to no females.

In rare quiet moments, Myra did sometimes wonder what a female dragon shifter would be like in real life. But then she remembered the dragon king, and how much of a pain in the ass he was, and thought better of her curiosity. A curiosity which as often as not got her into trouble. In this, though, she considered the common phrase "leave sleeping dragons lie" a good way to stay alive.

"Issa is human," Christopher said. "But she was involved romantically with a dragon shifter a few years ago. The relationship didn't take. They separated. But they'd had a child together. And it seems like her son is a dragon shifter."

More fascinating facts she hadn't known

before meeting him. That there were so many males running around the place because dragon shifters could produce offspring with humans. In fact, having a dragon shifter mother was apparently very very rare for most of the living dragon shifters. They almost all had one human parent. The dragon king himself had had a human mother. The king's age was a mystery he encouraged, but Myra knew he was old enough that his human mother had passed a long time ago. As far as she knew, his father had passed away also. But since that involved Christopher's family, she hadn't actually asked him about his grandparents yet. Or his own mother.

There were certain topics they just…seemed to avoid without making a conscious effort. Details about families had been one of those topics.

"Because he's a dragon," Christopher said, "he's entitled to an annuity from the king. Until he's old enough to start collecting his own hoard. He'll receive a dragon mentor to help him with all things shifter when he's old enough, too. Right now, he's only five and won't be ready to start shifting and flying for another five to ten years, depending on the youngling."

Myra listened in rapt fascination. Some of this she hadn't known. Like the fact that the king financially supported young shifters until they were old enough to strike out on their own. The insights into the more private aspects of the dragons were captivating. She didn't want to interrupt Christopher, even to ask a question, though she had many.

Primarily, what was Issa's problem that she was what Christopher considered a damsel in distress?

"The annuity means Issa can raise him comfortably while still affording school for her career change. Turns out the surgeons she works for are not great people. There are two partners, both of them arrogant, but one in particular is… difficult. Edgy, angry, abusive. She sometimes sexually harasses Issa and the other administrative staff, though she apparently doesn't do the same with the nurses. And her demands are beyond what can be expected of human beings to accomplish in any given time period."

"Sounds like a fun boss," Myra said, with a snort.

Christopher's tense mouth twitched. "There's a reason Issa is in college and planning a career move."

"Can't blame her. The other partner bad, too?"

"More indifferent to the bullying and harassment of his business partner. He sees his patients, makes a fortune, and leaves. Not concerning himself with the details of the business or the happiness of his employees."

"Lovely."

This time Christopher let out a full snort-laugh at her sarcastic assessment. "At any rate, Issa is often responsible for contacting insurance companies and working out copays for patients. They have an outside company that issues the actual bills, but she is involved in the practice's billing and insurance procedures." He let his gaze travel over the surrounding trees, most of them maple and oak so the branches were bare fingers of wood stretching toward the blue sky.

A small frown bunched his forehead and he held a finger to his mouth.

She glanced around, keeping quiet, looking for danger. A few minutes later, a small group passed, three adults and two kids. The kids were charging ahead of the adults, holding miniature binoculars, pointing noisily up into the trees. The adults, with cameras and their own binoculars hanging on straps around their necks, followed more slowly, smiling at the children and chatting quietly.

They didn't acknowledge Christopher and Myra, sitting a few feet away on the rocks, but one of the adults did glance their way briefly.

Once they'd passed, and Myra could no longer

hear the kids, she said quietly, "You heard them coming?" His shifter hearing was excellent.

"It isn't like anyone will know or understand what we're talking about," he said. "But I prefer to keep these details between us."

"Fair. I'm assuming the issue has to do with the surgery's billing practices."

Christopher's grin was quick and so sudden, Myra's heart started to thump harder. He had a very sexy smile. Something about the way his mouth curved…

She blinked when she realized her mind was wandering toward thoughts best left for when they weren't in public.

"You would be right in that assumption. Turns out the practice is…manipulating the bills so that the insurance companies are paying out for things that aren't being done, and patients are paying copays where they don't need to. All pretty subtle. If Issa hadn't been learning all about medical billing, she wouldn't have noticed the discrepancies."

"Has she gone to anyone? Talked to anyone?"

"She contacted the Department of Financial Services and the Health Department last week. Both have hotlines for suspected medical billing fraud and are supposedly confidential. The next day she came in to work, all the dodgy bills had been removed, patient records had been changed, and there was no sign of the evidence of fraud there'd been just two days before."

"Someone tipped off the partners and they cleaned up their books."

Christopher nodded. "Or at least, they hid the actual paper trail and subbed in false documents to make it look like things were on the up and up if their records were audited. Issa has no idea how they did that in just two days, but she suspects the evidence is still there. They haven't had enough time to fully cover up their fraud."

"This all sounds like something the various government agencies and their forensic auditors are supposed to deal with," she said hesitantly. "And Issa's filed reports were confidential, right? So no one in the office knows she was the whistleblower."

"Seems the same insider person who tipped the practice off to the fraud reports so they could clean up the paper trail also found out and revealed Issa's identity. The more difficult of the partners has fired Issa. And intends on making sure she can't get a job anywhere in the medical field in this city again."

"That sucks. Big time. All around. Issa should get a lawyer and sue." She paused. "But what does this have to do with you and me?" she finally asked. "What do you think we could do to help?"

"Issa knows the practice is still misbilling people and skimming money, and she strongly suspects some evidence of this is still inside the office because there really hasn't been time for the partners to erase everything. They got rid of the person they thought could tell what was and was not fraud, so now they'd have less reason to worry about hiding the evidence."

"Won't someone from the state be investigating them?"

"The fraud reports were closed, without investigation, marked as without sufficient evidence to pursue, even though they never really investigated Issa's claims."

"So whoever is helping inside the state and health departments is also part of the cover up?"

People went to an awful lot of trouble to make a few extra dollars. And her form of thievery was considered the "bad" kind. At least she was an honest thief who only stole from people who could afford to lose what she took.

"Seems likely," Christopher said.

"Still waiting to hear how you think we can help."

"I want to break in to the practice and get the evidence Issa needs. Then hand it over personally and officially to an investigator, as a representative of the king. So they can't afford to cover it up without causing a…diplomatic situation. Issa having a dragon son gives her status in our community, and puts her under the protection of the dragons. But I need the actual evidence or I'm just hollowly threatening public servants."

"A bad look."

He nodded.

"So. A little light breaking and entering. And you need a thief for that."

"It would help," he said with a shrug. "If you'd rather not, if this is too close to feeling like you're working for the king, I'll understand."

It might well be too close to working for the king. The king had obviously told Christopher about this knowing he'd want to help a single mother in distress. And that he'd tell Myra about the situation. Or maybe this was another test. To see if Christopher would tell her things not specifically meant for her. Maybe the king wanted to see what Myra would do for Christopher.

Unfortunately, what she'd do for Christopher went a lot farther than what she intended on doing for the king. No more working for the king. But helping Christopher when what he needed aligned with her particular skill set…

"Yeah, I'm going to help," she said with a little head shake. "Maybe I have a latent damsel in distress issue, too."

His mouth quirked up at one corner, the small smile making her giddy. "Either damsels in distress or dragons in distress. I'm still deciding."

"If the dragon is you... That makes a difference."

THREE

Before breaking into the plastic surgeons' practice, Myra wanted a meeting with Issa. If she had to look for evidence of medical billing fraud, she needed to know what she was looking for. And she wanted to take the measure of the woman. Someone who'd actually had a relationship with a dragon shifter, had a child with a dragon shifter. And now, even though she was no longer with that shifter, still kept ties with the dragons because of her son.

Myra didn't allow herself consciously to consider *why* she was interested in Issa's personal life and situation with the dragons. But she was… curious.

They met at a café on the Upper West Side, putting the entirety of Central Park between Issa and her former place of employment. And still she seemed antsy and jumpy, sitting at a table at the halfway point of the narrow coffee shop. Since this was one of the funky, independent businesses, and not a chain coffee store, the wooden tables and floors were delightfully scuffed, the walls covered in opera posters, displaying shows put on at the Met, and the counter and coffee was handled by two employees, one with extensive piercings and tattoos, the other with glasses and a tight, high bun.

Myra strongly suspected the two women were also in a romantic relationship based on the way they smiled and danced around each other. But her tendency to people-watch when in a coffee shop had to be curtailed. She did keep half an eye on the other three people in the place. A woman working on her laptop, and two men with their heads bent together as they talked quietly. Outside of the initial startled glances at Christopher—it was hard not to notice when a man nearly seven feet tall walked into a room—no one paid them any particular attention. Even the initial startlement was shrugged off quickly and everyone returned to what they were doing with no more attention paid to him.

Myra loved New York and New Yorkers.

"They are definitely still embezzling," Issa

said, as she toyed with her coffee cup, circling it between her hands without sipping on it. Plain black coffee in a bowl-shaped ceramic mug with a pithy saying on the side. She'd refused a pastry.

Myra had not refused a pastry—fruit and cream filled tart that was delicately flaky and not too sweet—and her coffee was a cappuccino with a lot of yummy foam on top.

"Before I was let go," Issa said, "I saw at least one more bill for a current client that wasn't right. But I wasn't given time to look at it closely before Dr. Butler fired me. But if that bill hadn't been disposed of like the others I'd actually reported on, I'm sure there are more in the office still. Dr. Butler thinks she's smarter than she is."

This last was said with a snarl as Issa glanced down into her cooling coffee.

Issa Abarca was a tall woman, thick and curvy, with black hair she currently had twisted into a series of braids held up in a bun. Under soft, subtle makeup, there was a scattering of freckles across her pale tan nose. The makeup didn't hide the circles under her dark eyes, or the worry lines bracketing her mouth. Myra guessed her to be somewhere in her mid-thirties.

Not for the first time since they'd sat down, Issa pressed a finger to her left eye, rubbing gently. Myra couldn't tell if it was a nervous tic or if Issa had something in her eye.

When Issa looked up and noticed Myra watching her, she said, "I've got something in my contact lens. Can't seem to get it out." She shrugged. "I'll rinse it later."

"How far back does the embezzlement go?" Christopher asked, quietly. He'd slouched a little in his seat, the wood creaking under his weight, but Issa didn't seem to be bothered by his height. She hadn't given him that double take that people often did.

The reaction made Myra wonder if it was just that Issa was used to dragon shifters or if she and Christopher had met before. Christopher hadn't mentioned it if they had.

"I'm not sure," Issa said. "A few years. Maybe more. But I only noticed the discrepancies in the last eight months of billing, so maybe less?" She shook her head and rubbed lightly at the edge of her left eye again. "I have a kid to look after. And my tuition for the next semester took out my reserves. I only have this one semester left. But…" She closed her eyes briefly. "I've spent all this money to get this degree, so I can do a different job. And now I might not be able to get a job in the field because of a crook." She sighed. "I don't want to move. My son's father lives here.

They're close. I don't want to screw that up. But if I can't work…" She spread her hands around her coffee mug before gripping it tight again.

"Is Dr. Butler's partner involved in the embezzlement?" Myra asked. "Or does he just go along for the ride?"

"His billing seems standard. I never saw anything suspicious there. Doesn't necessarily mean anything. He profits from his partner's actions." She tugged at her left eye again and cursed quietly. "Sorry, I'll be right back. I have to get this rinsed."

She stood, taking her purse with her, and headed to the back of the narrow coffee shop, weaving past the table with the two men talking to reach the single bathroom.

Myra watched her go, frowning a little when she turned back to Christopher. "What do you think?"

"I think she needs help, and I think she doesn't know what to do next."

"Agreed. And I think she's telling the truth." Which wasn't always the case with people Myra encountered in her line of work.

The door to the coffee shop opened on a dinging bell as another customer walked in.

Christopher lowered his voice so that it was difficult to hear him over the sounds of the espresso machine. "I'm not sure we'll find what she's looking for at the offices, though. Knowing one of their employees figured out the embezzlement scam means Dr. Butler might be more careful for the next few months."

"Maybe. But it also sounds like she's pretty arrogant. And thinks she's covered by whoever she knows at the Health Department or Department of Financial Services that warned her about the whistleblower report. People like that don't tend to cover their trail as well as they think they do." Myra leaned back in her chair. It did not creak the way it did under Christopher's weight. "I'll start at the practice offices. If I can't find anything there, we can always try Dr. Bulter's home."

"Don't write off her partner either," Christopher said. "If he's okay with Butler's crimes, he might be okay with helping her cover them up."

"Fair point." Myra frowned at the still closed bathroom door. "Would Issa be able to move, to get a job, given who her son is related to? She said she didn't want to, but…would your father, or her son's father, try to stop the move? Is there…a legal issue with her moving?"

"No more so than if the boy's father were human. It depends on the custody arrangement they have. My father might…discourage a move. Having loyal dragons in his immediate territory is good for his power base. If Issa moves for work and takes her son into another dragon king's territory, it would be possible her son would shift loyalties to that new king. But my father can't legally prevent her from moving."

"She didn't sound like she wanted to."

"She shouldn't have to because an embezzler blackballed her."

"Agreed. So we'll break into the office first, then if nothing there, we'll try other avenues of tracking down evidence." Myra tapped her fingers against the wooden table top, running her short fingernails in a tipping pattern as she thought. "But once we have the evidence, what do we do with it? We can't turn it over to the very people who are already covering for Dr. Butler. I know you said you'd put the weight of the dragons behind a formal report but that doesn't stop Butler from interfering in Issa's job prospects. How do we get the woman to leave Issa and her career alone? Do we actually do anything to stop Butler's scam? Or are we just getting the evidence to use as…blackmail to make the good doctor back off?"

She glanced away from the bathroom to look at Christopher. He was frowning, his forehead bunched into creases she had the irrational urge to smooth with her fingertips.

"I think we let Issa decide what to do with the evidence," Christopher said. "It's her life, her future. She should decide how she wants to proceed."

Myra smiled as Christopher's gaze swept down to her. "Good plan."

The bathroom door finally opened and Issa came out, blinking a few times. She gave Myra a little smile on the way back to their table.

But before she reached them, the two men who'd been sitting with their heads together, talking quietly, stood suddenly, blocking Issa.

For a split second, Myra just assumed they were rude, getting up to leave and not paying any attention to the people around them.

Then she saw the gun in one's hand. The widened, panicked look in Issa's dark eyes.

And before Myra could even push her chair back, the man with the gun had his arm wrapped around Issa's neck, the gun at her temple, using her as a shield in front of him.

His companion stood behind him, also with a gun. His pointed at Christopher.

"Don't try anything," the man with the gun at Issa's temple said. "Or we'll kill her."

Myra raised her hands, palms facing the men. "What do you want?"

"We're taking the woman for a little chat with our boss. You want her released alive, you'll look out for a message."

"Ransom," Myra said, rising slowly.

The second man, whose gun had been aimed at Christopher, shifted the barrel to point the gun at her.

She kept her hands raised and her gaze on Issa and the gunman behind her, trusting Christopher to watch the second man. "Who do you think she has to pay a random? She's just a single mom. Working hard. Just been fired. There isn't money for a ransom."

The man snorted. "Boss knows who her son's father is." He flicked a glance at Christopher. "What that connects her to. You want her alive? You want her to see her son again? You back off looking into the boss's business, and you make sure that ransom gets paid when you get it. No tricks." He glanced at the side of Issa's face. "Shame for her son if his mother was killed."

Issa's eyes widened, her skin paled, her hands were visibly shaking, and her breath came in such hard, fast gulps, Myra worried she'd pass out. Her bottom lip quivered and she looked like she wanted to scream, to cry, to say something. But she remained silent and trembling and staring at Myra with such desperation in her gaze, Myra's own hands twitched to reach out to her.

The two gunmen eased around the narrow path between tables, keeping Issa between Myra and Christopher and themselves. The second man kept his gun trained toward Myra and Christopher. The first never moved his from Issa's temple.

Tears tracked down Issa's cheeks as they reached the front door.

The two women behind the counter had ducked down, out of view. The woman on her lap top had folded herself into the corner, using her table and laptop as cover. The silence in the café was broken only by Issa's quiet whimpers and the sudden sound of the coffee machine grinder going on.

"Call the cops on us," the man said, "and she's dead. Just do as instructed, she'll live to see her son again."

They backed out of the café's glass door, onto the busy sidewalk. Half a dozen people screamed at the sight of the guns. A few walked past without even noticing. A black SUV pulled up onto the sidewalk, which drew almost as many gasped and outraged yells and screams as the two men with guns. The back door opened and the two gunmen pushed Issa inside before jumping in behind her.

By the time Myra and Christopher reached the sidewalk, the SUV had sped away, racing up the avenue, honking and whipping around the rest of traffic, running a red light. It screeched around a corner. Disappearing from sight.

Myra glanced at Christopher. He stripped his shirt off without a word. She jumped into his arms as his shirt dropped to the sidewalk and his wings snapped open behind him.

They were airborne an instant later, leaving the sounds of more shouting and gasps on the sidewalk below.

So much for being inconspicuous.

FOUR

Christopher banked, following the road below, keeping the black SUV in sight as it sped through the streets of the Upper West Side, and launch up the West Side Highway. The cold afternoon air whipped across Myra's cheeks. Christopher was flying fast enough the rush of air made her eyes water. She clung to his neck, but kept her gaze on the SUV. Afraid if she looked away too long, she'd lose it in the traffic.

And with it, Issa.

"They'll know you can follow this way, won't they?" she asked, speaking loudly to be heard above the rushing air and the noise of protesting traffic below. "They knew about Issa's connection to the dragons even without saying it aloud."

"They might know," he acknowledged. "But will rightly assume we won't try anything while they have guns on Issa."

"What are we going to do?" she asked. She was a thief not an expert in rescuing kidnap victims.

Though, technically, that's what she'd done with Christopher. She'd reframed it in her mind, though, to fit her skill set. She'd gone in and stolen him back from his kidnappers. She could steal things. That's what she *did*.

Rescuing people on the other hand…

"First, we make sure we know where they're going. Then we get Issa back."

Christopher's voice was hard, and very deep, and that underlying, inhuman hissing growl was there under his words.

"We could just pay the ransom and then I can steal the money back after Issa is safe," Myra suggested. "Your father would front the money, right?"

"That's what they're counting on."

Yeah, Myra sort of thought so, too. Especially after they specifically referenced who Issa's son was related to and glanced at Christopher. They knew the boy's father was a dragon shifter and that by extension that meant the dragon king would be involved in the situation. The dragon king had more than enough money to pay a ransom, even a big one.

The question was, would the king *really* pay the ransom for one random human woman?

The boy's father was still around. The boy's father was a dragon shifter. The king might *want* the boy to be raised by his father, away from human influence.

Though, if that were the case, he probably wouldn't have "mentioned" Issa's problem to Christopher, knowing Christopher would want to save her.

The SUV headed down the West Side Highway, barreling through the snarl of cars, shoving them aside physically to get them to move if it had to. The time of day was leading into rush hour, so things were starting to get heavy, but not as bad as they'd been in about an hour.

"They're heading to the tunnel," Myra said.

It was a ways to go downtown to reach the Lincoln Tunnel. Going up to the George Washington would have been a lot closer from where they'd started. But on this route, short of heading into some specific place in Lower Manhattan, she couldn't imagine where else the SUV would be going.

They'd hardly stay in Manhattan where the

king and his dragons could more easily hunt them down.

There were a lot of places in New Jersey for a black SUV to disappear. The king's sway in the state wasn't as powerful as in New York. And she and Christopher would lose that specific car in the tunnel since Christopher couldn't safely fly *through* the tunnel.

"Do we stop them before they reach it?" she asked.

"If we try to, they might just shoot Issa."

"Can we land on the car and…ride through the tunnel that way?"

"They realize we're there, they'll shoot up through the car. Or shoot Issa."

"We're fucked if they make the tunnel."

Christopher banked low, so close to the roofs of the cars, Myra actually gasped and clung tighter to his neck. Usually, he stayed well above traffic when he flew her around the city, often above the buildings. From that height, the only thing they were likely to hit was an errant flock of birds.

This close to the cars, the possibility of electrical and phone wires, or even big delivery trucks, felt a lot more imminent.

She didn't close her eyes when he flew directly up to, then whipped around a large delivery van, but she did have to press her teeth together so she didn't squeal.

A giddy rush of adrenaline hit her bloodstream hard. And it took a great deal of effort for Myra to hold in her laughter. This wasn't a laughing situation. Issa's life was on the line.

But hot damn the rush in this kind of danger…

Christopher swung up behind the SUV, close enough Myra could see into the back windows, see Issa's head bracketed by the two men from the café through the dark tinting. There had to be at least two more people in the SUV. The driver, and whoever had opened the back door for the gunmen and Issa to get into the car. But Myra couldn't see either of those two people from this vantage.

What she could clearly see was the SUV's plates.

"Got the number." Christopher gave his wings a heavy downward sweep and heaved them higher above the cars again.

The change in direction and sudden rise making her stomach drop and an edge of nausea clench around her middle before everything but the adrenaline rush settled.

"Now what?" she said as they went back to trailing the SUV from a higher altitude, skimming over the tops of wires, and reaching a height that felt less like they might run into a bridge or big truck.

"Now, we follow at a more discrete height and let them believe they've lost me in the tunnel."

"Your eyesight that good?"

"Yes."

That was scary. "Is that how you always manage to find me?"

He paused long enough she wondered if he'd even answer. Then, "Sometimes. But not always."

He had found her when she wasn't out in the open more than once. So she knew his scary good eyesight couldn't explain it all. She'd even searched herself for a tracking device at one stage. Nothing. Christopher just had an uncanny knack for finding her, no matter where she was. It would probably be more disconcerting if she didn't enjoy the moments when he did find her.

"You ever going to explain the times that have nothing to do with your eyesight?" she asked.

"One day. But not while we're chasing a woman in danger."

Well. That was fair enough.

FIVE

Christopher banked out over the Hudson as the SUV disappeared into the line of cars inching into the Lincoln Tunnel. Below them, ferries and tourist boats chugged down the slow, dirty water of the river, neatly avoiding the smaller sailboats and occasional fishing boat or kayak.

How people went kayaking in this weather was beyond Myra. Even when she wasn't mid-flight, the winter weather was frosty. Out over the water, the temperature dropped another few degrees. The thought of being that close to cold water made her shiver.

"You're cold," Christopher said.

She shook her head. "You're pumping out

enough body heat to keep me warm." His skin felt like he'd just come in from sitting in the sun, the scattering of purple and yellow scales over his shoulders and chest radiating heat.

While she'd read that ordinary dragons, what few were left, could be cold blooded and therefore needed quite a lot of heat to warm their huge bodies, dragon shifters, even in dragon form, were warm blooded. She got the feeling from Christopher that they could control that body heat better than the average mammal, warming themselves up when they needed to. Or when their emotions got the better of them.

Helped keep her warm midflight, too.

"I was thinking it's too cold to go kayaking," she explained.

"I have to agree." He adjusted his arms around her, lifting her a little closer to his body, and she tightened her hold on his neck.

"Am I getting too heavy?"

He glanced briefly down at her, his brows lifted in such a smugly sardonic expression, she rolled her eyes.

Since he'd once flown her from the back of a train all the way to Chicago, a flight that had taken hours, she realized her question was silly. Still, she felt rude not asking.

He took a flight path that circled them around

to the far side of the tunnel, where cars were rushing out onto the more open Jersey freeways.

"There are hundreds of black SUVs down there," she said with a sigh. "Not a bad plan, disappearing through the tunnel. Hopefully they don't know how good your eyesight is."

"We'll know soon. There they are."

He stayed high, gliding over the SUV as it moved toward Hoboken. The car had slowed to a reasonable speed, keeping pace with traffic now instead of ramming through and rushing past other cars. From above, it looked like every other car driving along the freeway, nothing to make it stand out. Even the dents on the front, where it had rammed other vehicles to move them out of its way during the earlier chase didn't stand out as particularly obvious because, even at this height, Myra spotted at least two other vehicles with damage.

This was why she mostly stuck to the subways. Cars were a menace.

The SUV eased off the freeway and headed into a residential area. Myra half expected them to drive to one of the many houses that looked like doll houses below her, but the SUV kept driving, moving from the residential area into a more industrial part of the city, where warehouses took up large swaths of marshy land, the shades of grays broken up by the occasional winter-brown tree planted along a sidewalk.

They watched the SUV pull into one of the industrial complexes, with a series of gray-white buildings scattered around empty parking lots. The car drove to one of the far buildings, a smaller one with large loading bay doors. The lot and building looked empty. There weren't even any trailers parked at the loading bays.

Christopher circled down to a flat rooftop with a low retaining wall that looked across to the building but was far enough away, the kidnappers would have to have excellent eyesight to see them. He got them onto the roof and they both ducked low to the retaining wall before anyone even stepped out of the SUV.

The driver was first, getting out and scanning their surroundings as he closed the car door. They were much too far away for her to see him clearly or to hear anything that was said, so she asked Christopher, "He have a gun, too?"

Christopher nodded without speaking, his eyes narrowed.

After a moment of scanning, the driver opened the back door, keeping his gaze on the surroundings as he let the people in the back out. First came one of the men from the café. The taller of the two, the one who'd kept his gun trained on Myra and Christopher.

He was taller than the driver as well as the other gunman, but only by a few inches, and leaner than the driver, who was wide shouldered and thick through the middle. Both men were white and had dark hair, but that was the best she could do at a distance. Her memory of the two men in the café was that they'd been ordinary looking. Dressed casually in jeans, with their black coats still on as they'd hunched over their table talking. Since she hadn't bothered to take her jacket off inside the coffee shop either, she had noted the coats but not found it particularly suspicious. It really was cold outside.

No obvious external features to the two men either to make them stand out. Neither even wore glasses. And she hadn't noticed any obvious jewelry, which was something she did make note of on all the people around her, though usually subconsciously.

Old habits.

Issa was next out of the car. She stumbled a little when she hit the ground, and the man who'd gotten out first braced her with a hand on her arm. He dropped his touch the minute she got her balance and jerked free, then stepped to one side so she could move out of the way for the last man in the back seat.

Who climbed out still holding his gun in his hand.

As far as Myra could tell, neither of the other men had weapons in their hands. But Christopher had confirmed even the driver had a gun.

Lot of guns between them and Issa. And Myra was pretty sure Christopher wasn't bulletproof. She definitely wasn't bulletproof.

She hated guns.

Reaching inside the multi-pocketed vest under her coat, she pulled out a tiny pair of binoculars.

"Is there anything you don't carry inside that vest?" Christopher asked as she set the binoculars to her eyes.

"Nothing that might be useful."

"Binoculars are regularly useful?"

"In my job? Yes. All the time."

She felt more than saw his head tilt in a shrug.

Scanning the men and Issa briefly, she confirmed Issa didn't appear injured. In fact, now that they were all out of the car and walking toward the building, none of the men even touched her. The first man from the coffee shop who'd taken her hostage walked behind her with a gun pointed at her back, but that was the only method of restraint. No cuffs or ties. Nothing to keep her from screaming. Though out here, with no signs of life anywhere nearby, screaming probably would seem pointless.

Myra swung her binoculars back to the SUV. She was certain there was at least one more person in that car. Someone had to have opened the back door. The driver couldn't have. But only the three men and Issa had gotten out.

"There's someone still in the car," she said. With the magnified vision, she could barely see movement inside the tinted windows. A changing of light coming through the windshields to indicate the car wasn't empty. The SUV was parked in the shadows of the building, so there wasn't enough light hitting the windows to light up whoever was inside.

"Can you see them?" she asked Christopher with his superior eyesight.

"One person, no one else, but I can't tell much more about them. Tint has something in it that's distorting my vision."

That was interesting. He could see into the car, but not as clearly as he might be able to without the tint. That there was a way to tint car windows that affected dragon shifter eyesight was a new fact for her. Something else to research.

She swung her binoculars back to the quartet as they headed inside the building, climbing a short set of metal stairs to a door that had an obvious lock panel beside the doorknob. The driver entered a code, waited a beat, then turned the knob and opened the door wide enough to let the other two men and Issa proceed him inside. He continually scanned his surroundings as he waited for them to pass, only taking his gaze off the lot and other buildings when he finally ducked inside and the door closed.

"Code lock but no cards or keys or biometrics," she murmured.

"You can handle that?"

"I can handle that."

"Good. Smashing in the door would be too noisy. Give away our element of surprise."

She lowered the binoculars to look at the side of his face. The door in question was thick and metal and looked pretty substantial. "You could smash in that door?"

"I could smash in that door," he said without glancing at her.

"Not sure if I'm impressed or appalled." He was very strong. No wonder he'd looked at her like she was ridiculous when she'd asked if she was getting too heavy.

"The person in the SUV getting out?" she asked as she swung her binoculars back to the car.

"No. But there's another vehicle coming."

"There is?" She lowered her binoculars again to scan the area. She could hear traffic and cars in the distance as a low drone of background noise amidst the quieter hum of wind around the industrial park. But now that she paid attention, she could hear a more distinct motor separating from the distant background drone.

Sure enough, a heavy engine sports car motored around the corner of a building, growling up to the SUV. Pretty and red but that was the best Myra could do. She did not specialize in stealing sportscars, so they weren't in her expertise.

The sportscar parked on the far side of the SUV, doors opened and closed. Even with her binoculars, she couldn't see who had gotten out until they came around the back of the SUV. At which point, the driver of the little red sportscar revealed himself to be a medium height, middle aged man, his head shaven, his beard scruff artful, his skin artificially tan, and his short-sleeved polo shirt entirely inappropriate for the weather. He looked irritated as all hell, pointing at someone still hidden behind the SUV, and speaking loudly enough Myra could almost hear him.

"What's he saying?" she asked Christopher without taking her eyes off the man. Through the binoculars, he was easy enough to see but not someone she recognized.

"He's yelling at the person behind the car about getting him involved in all this. It's their fault. He's an innocent bystander. Blah blah blah."

Myra pressed her lips together to keep from laughing. Her huge dragon shifter companion saying, "blah blah blah," struck her as remarkably funny for some reason. Also, his obvious annoyance with the newcomer couldn't have been clearer.

"Do you recognize him?" she asked.

"No. But I will bet that's the second doctor from the practice Issa worked at."

"Not taking that bet. I think you're right." She watched for a moment more before saying, "What do you bet the person we can't see, the remaining person in the SUV, is Dr. Butler?"

"I'd bet my father's hoard."

She grinned. "Not your hoard, of course."

"Of course not."

The absolute afront in his response did have her quietly chuckling.

They watched another minute, with the sportscar man continuing to yell, before the person he was yelling at finally came into view.

And the absolutely stunning woman that stepped up to him, with strappy black heels so high they made Myra dizzy and an elegant sweep of jet black hair, struck the man silent.

The woman wore very dark sunglasses, so Myra couldn't see her eyes. But even at a distance, it was obvious she was a beautiful woman. Slim, dressed in a long white coat that wrapped snuggly around her small waist, her long legs encased in stockings that sparkled in the winter light. Even her hair looked glossy and perfect.

For a moment, Myra had this odd feeling that the woman was not real. That she had stepped out of a magazine, airbrushing and all, to exist in the real world and yet not be of the real world.

The woman stepped up very close to the man who had, just moments ago, been blustering and yelling at her, and he lowered his head as she got near. She stuck her finger under his chin, lifting his head, but he still didn't meet her gaze.

Through the binoculars, Myra could see the woman's lips move, close to the man's face. "Can you hear her?" she asked Christopher. There was no hope of her hearing the woman. All she heard was the whistle of a sudden gust of wind through the complex.

She felt more than saw Christopher shake his head. "She's speaking too quietly. Whispering. I get the sound, but not the words."

"That you even get the sound is impressive."

After a moment of this whispering, the woman stepped away from the man, the man lowered his head again, looking properly chastised, and the woman smoothed a hand down her coat before gesturing at the door where the gunmen and Issa had gone. The man nodded his head rapidly, then extended and arm for the woman to proceed him which she did.

The whole thing couldn't have lasted more than two minutes. But it felt like Myra had just watched a fully half hour drama in those minutes.

Once the woman and man—presumably Dr. Butler and her practice partner—had disappeared inside, Myra lowered her binoculars and scanned their surroundings. The area was silent now, no more cars growling into the lot. Just the distant sound of traffic and the whistling breeze.

"See anyone else?" she checked with Christopher and his superior eyesight and hearing.

He shook his head, then stood and let his wings unfurl from where he'd kept them tight to his back while crouched out of sight. "Can you open that door quickly?"

"I can open that door quickly. But let's see if we can find a window first. I want to know what the interior of the warehouse looks like."

"Issa might not have that kind of time."

Myra was worried about that too. "If we see or hear anything, we can always go crashing in through a window. Create some chaos."

She tucked her little binoculars away into their pocket, and without a word, jumped up into Christopher's arms. He swept them up into the air an instant later, as if they'd practice this move so often it was habit, well trained muscle memory.

For reasons, that made Myra all soft and giddy inside.

Six

They swept around the perimeter of the building, gliding on a cushion of air just above the ground. There were a few windows high up on the two story structure, but when Christopher flew close enough for them to see inside, all Myra could see were stacks of wooden and metal crates.

Anxiety and worry for Issa clawed at her gut, and she suspected Christopher was impatient to get inside and rescue Issa, too. But he'd been kidnapped once when he rushed into a situation to rescue a damsel in distress. Myra refused to be responsible for him getting kidnapped again, or worse, because they didn't know what the situation was inside that warehouse.

The situation inside, however, was something

they'd only figure out once she got them through the code lock on the door.

He set them down gently at the top of the staircase, his feet settling onto the metal so lightly, he didn't make noise. Given he'd made the wooden chair in the coffee shop groan, Myra was impressed.

The code lock took her about twenty seconds and she used a spell to do it because they didn't have the extra ten seconds she would have needed using an old school heat scanner to pick up the buttons that had been recently pushed. The spell basically did the same thing, lighting up the buttons pressed, and there were enough of them for the type of lock she was looking at to indicate no repeat numbers.

The lock snicked open, but Myra stopped Christopher before he rushed in. She eased the door just wide enough to listen to what was happening beyond. When she couldn't hear anything immediately, she crept inside, taking in her immediate surroundings with a sweep of her gaze.

Red painted metal stairs leading back down to ground level. Blue concrete floors. Boxes and wooden crates piled on the floor. A few stacks of larger, metal shipping crates. It wasn't a giant building, but was tall enough for the shipping crates to stack two high.

She eased down the metal staircase, and headed immediately to the cover of a nearby stack of wooden boxes.

Christopher leapt from the stairs landing right beside her behind the crates, hitting the ground with the lightness of a cat.

She rolled her eyes. Show off.

She touched her ear with a finger and narrowed her eyes up at him. He gave a brief nod and headed in one direction. She followed, quietly, trusting his hearing to pinpoint the location of everyone.

That she trusted him, anyone really, to guide her through the building was a revelation. She trusted Christopher to catch her when she fell. She trusted him to lead her in the right direction in intense circumstances. She...trusted him. At least with her physical safety.

Unprecedented.

They stayed behind cover, easing through the warehouse. Reaching a point where even Myra could hear voices. A quiet whispering female voice. Issa's denials. A man lifting his voice in an almost shout before he also quieted.

As they neared, the words got clearer.

"You shouldn't have brought the dragon king into all this," the woman said.

"I didn't." Issa, sounding like she wanted to cry. "I just told Havier I would have to move after Dr. Butler fired me. He informed the king. I didn't do anything."

Myra frowned. She'd been assuming the woman was Dr. Butler and the man was Dr. Butler's partner. But… Something about the way Issa mentioned Butler made it sound like she was referring to someone else completely. Not the woman with the quiet voice who'd shut the sportscar man up with a look.

Okay. So. Something more going on here. And not just two people trying to shut up a whistleblower.

Somewhere around here, there were also the three gunmen.

"I told you," a man said. "I told you this was a bad idea."

Myra guessed that was the sportscar man, but couldn't see him yet to be sure.

"The king sent his son," the woman said. "His son would have found out everything. This wasn't a situation I could let go."

"What could they do? She destroyed everything. All the evidence is gone."

"And the king's pet thief? You don't think she'd have found anything?"

Pet thief? Myra mouthed at Christopher, her scowl fierce.

That was *exactly* what she'd been afraid of. People starting to think she somehow *belonged* to the king and his cohort just because she'd done a few jobs for him. Bad enough the *king* had started to think that. Other people thinking that was both bad *and* wrong.

Probably the fact that she was…on her way to being…romantically involved with the king's son didn't help that perception, but that was another issue. As was her stuttering over what to call her relationship with Christopher.

"There's nothing for her to find," the man insisted. "But now you've made things worse! Kidnapped a woman in broad daylight. While she was with those two. They'll find us. The king will know. The police will know."

"My men lost the king's son. He's not some sort of omnipresent god. None of them are. Despite what the king would have people believe."

Wow. Sounded like there was some history there. But also, hadn't the woman heard of license plate numbers?

"I won't stand by for this. We can't just kill

her. The police will come looking at our practice first. They'll *know*. They'll figure it out."

Shit. Okay. Wanting to kill Issa was bad. Issa's quiet whimper and plea for her life after that didn't help.

"I have a son," she said brokenly. "Please. He needs me."

Heat pumped off Christopher from Myra's side, his anger obvious even without having to look at him. She set her hand against his arm to keep him from rushing in and it was a bit like touching a fire. Not quite hot enough to burn. But since they weren't flying and they weren't outside in the cold air, the heat felt like it would burn if he got much hotter.

She understood the reaction. She wanted to run in and rescue Issa, too. Had wanted to since she'd first been kidnapped. But there were still those three gunmen.

Given the conversation, Myra was now certain the man talking was the sportscar man, and he'd confirmed he was Dr. Butler's partner. Where the hell Dr. Butler was was a hanging question. But they could sort that out after they got Issa out of this. Hopefully without Christopher lighting the whole place on fire.

Against Chrisopher's ear, in a whisper so quiet, she wasn't even sure she was speaking aloud, she said, "We have to see what's happening. The gunmen."

He jerked his chin in a nod. When she leaned back to look at him, his jaw was set, his eyes fairly glowing in the dark, a yellow glow over the blue, and he looked like he could chew rocks.

But instead of running headlong into the situation, he tapped his nose.

She assumed that meant he could smell something important.

Then he pointed to their left and right.

Okay. She was going to interpret that as where the gunmen were. She mouthed, *gunmen*? Just to be sure.

Another jerky nod.

So. One to their left and one to their right at least. But the third had to be with Issa. Either that, or the woman had a gun they hadn't seen earlier.

Christopher leaned in close to whisper in her ear. It was like stepping up to the very edge of a bonfire. "I'll take care of the two gunmen not with the group. Be right back."

Before she could stop him, he was gone, moving so fast she blinked. Shit.

She knew, because he was a shapeshifter, because he was a dragon, he could move very fast when he wanted to. She'd flown with him at speed. But this was the first time she'd really seen him move so fast she'd been unable to visually follow him.

The realization he could do that was disorienting.

More disorienting was how fast he returned.

She blinked up at him. *Are they dead?* she mouthed.

Brief head shake. "Unconscious," he whispered against her ear. "Guns destroyed."

He'd done all that and done it in complete silence? In less than a minute. Woah.

Okay. Maybe they could get Issa out alive after all.

She motioned him to the left, so they could move around the crates and get a view of the situation around Issa. The remaining group were still talking, with the man arguing with the woman in quiet but intense tones and Issa quietly crying. The sound of her soft sobs went right through Myra. She could only imagine how bad this was for Christopher.

They reached a spot where, with a quick glance around one of the metal shipping crates, Myra could see the group. The woman, the sportscar man, the remaining gunman, and Issa on her knees at the center of them all. The gunman had his gun pointed at the back of Issa's head.

They needed a distraction for the gunman.

Christopher, with his apparent super speed, could race in there and remove Issa from the middle of the group, but not if the gunman startled and got a shot off first. Even if he missed Issa's head, he'd hit…someone.

Myra pointed to the metal crate. Mouthed, *I'm going up.*

Christopher scowled at her.

Distraction.

More scowling. She wasn't sure if the scowl was because he didn't understand or because he didn't want her to be the distraction. He didn't have much choice if it was the latter, but if the former…

You, go in and get Issa. She made gestures to emphasize her mouthed words, hoping he got it. *I'll make sure the gun is pointing somewhere else.*

This would be easier if she could just say the words to him, but they were so close to the others now, she didn't want to risk it. Reading lips, even with careful enunciation, still left room for error.

She tried a final time since Christopher was still scowling at her. *You…* She pointed at his chest. *Get Issa. I…* She pointed at her chest. *Will distract the others.*

No.

She wasn't entirely sure what he was noing. Him going in to rescue Issa or her distracting the others so he could. She had a feeling it was the latter, though, because this was Christopher after all.

She grinned at him and pointed upward. *Be back soon. Don't miss your opening.*

And just because she felt like it, because he was pumping off heat like a boiler and looked so fierce and angry, she rose up on her toes and kissed him. Light and quick. On the mouth. Then spun around the back of the crate before he could stop her.

Technically, she thought as she found the ladder up to the top of the metal shipping crate, he probably could still stop her. Given he could move in a blink. She hoped he'd trust her to do her part as she was trusting him to do his. This was a team effort here.

That she was working with anyone else, even one other person, was astonishing.

That she didn't mind…

Unprecedented.

SEVEN

Myra shimmied up the flat ladder stuck to the side of the metal shipping crate, careful of her footing and ensuring she made no sounds. The roof of the crate was tricker, inclined to bend and creak if she wasn't careful. That would work for her, but she needed to time things right.

Below her, the woman was still lecturing the sportscar man about how he'd fucked everything up. The sportscar man was arguing that they couldn't afford any more bodies on their hands. And since Issa had whistleblown on embezzlement and not murder, the fact that there were *more* bodies involved was news.

Issa remained on her knees in the middle of the group, quietly sobbing into her hands, her face covered. At the mention of *more* bodies, she shivered hard and shrank farther in on herself. The gunman stood behind her, his gun pointed at her head, his attention on the man and woman yelling at each other, his expression bored.

Unfortunately, for all the boredom, he didn't look like he was going to point the gun elsewhere or drop his arm any time soon.

Somewhere below and hidden, Christopher waited, pumping off so much heat in his anger, Myra worried he'd melt the side of the shipping container.

The lights inside the warehouse were dim in most sections but bright enough in this part of the space Myra had to be careful she didn't cast shadows from her perch up on top of the shipping crate, so she kept low, inching over the metal to get into position.

"The king will come after us for sure if you do this," the sportscar man hissed. His artificially tan skin looked pale and pasty in the bright overhead lights. His bald head was dotted with sweat even though it wasn't that warm inside and he was still only wearing a polo shirt.

That the partner was here but not Dr. Butler had Myra pretty curious, since Butler was the one whose supposed embezzlement had led to all this.

"Her son is a dragon," sportscar man said, flinging a hand at Issa. Issa flinched.

"And he has a dragon father who will take care of him," the woman said dryly. "The king will probably prefer that anyway."

This close, it was easier to see the woman's flawless complexion, smooth and pale under expert makeup. Her black hair, twisted into an elegant bun. The spikey heels she stood on looking even higher and spikier up close. Myra would definitely break an ankle on those.

The woman hadn't loosened her white coat yet, so it was still wrapped around her like a dress. Her sparkling nylons gave her long legs a sheen that weirdly reminded Myra of the way Christopher's scales caught the light when he did his partial shift. A sort of soft sparkle. But Christopher's scales were purple and yellow. The woman's nylons were an ordinary tan color.

Her age was just as difficult to pinpoint this close up. That vaguely mid-thirties sort of age that could mean she was anything from a mature-looking twenty year old or a well-preserved fifty year old. The woman's body posture and clothing screamed money to Myra—who was used to assessing these things—a kind of casual wealth that still, nevertheless, wanted people to know she was wealthy.

Lot of old money people dressed in ordinary clothes, ripped jeans and worn t-shirts and, depending, expensive converse or inexpensive wellies. Old money, the ones secure in their wealth and station in life, tended to show up in the world like ordinary people, with a few hints that the money was there in the background.

People who wanted people to know they were wealthy, people who *needed* others to know they were rich, always looked the part.

And made great marks for people like Myra.

This woman, though… Myra was having trouble reading her. It was like this obvious wealthy appearance was a sort of act. A costume she'd donned for a point. Myra couldn't even say what details about her were making Myra assume that. Outwardly, she seemed to be exactly what she was. But Myra was used to studying people, their dress, their body language.

Something about the woman wasn't adding up.

"Please," Issa sobbed into her hands. "My son needs me."

The woman glared down at Issa's bent head. "Sons do not need their mothers that desperately, woman. You should consider that falsehood. Dragon sons need their own people. But not their mothers."

Myra narrowed her eyes. Yeah. Something was definitely up with that woman. She knew an awful lot about dragon shifters, and had some very specific opinions.

Who the hell was she?

Whoever she was, it was time to get Issa away from her. And the man with the gun pointing at Issa's head.

Myra lifted her head a little more, a darting motion before she lowered back to the container roof. She shifted to the left. The metal roof creaked.

"Someone's here," the gunman said. The first time he'd spoken.

The woman's eyes narrowed and she lifted her head.

Myra lifted enough to be seen again, dropping as fast. A quick sort of motion. Like someone trying to avoid being seen.

Then moved slightly right. Another creak on the metal roof.

The sound of a gun firing was so loud in the confined space, Myra covered her ears when she ducked. Though the sound came at the same time as the bullet whizzed over her head.

"Up there," the woman shouted. "It's the thief. Get her!"

Nice to be recognized?

No. Myra did not like that the woman had recognized her at all.

She crab-walked backward along the metal roof as more shots rang out over her head and more shouting came from the group below.

She realized they expected the other two men to hurry to them, or at least expected the other two men to be there. Using that, she slithered down the side of the shipping container and made an obvious dart between it and another pile of boxes moving in the direction where one of the now disabled men had been.

Hoping when Christopher had left him unconscious, he done a thorough enough job the man wasn't already getting to his feet. And that Christopher had checked for more than the one weapon.

More bullets. Ricocheting off the metal containers. Thunking heavily into the wooden crates. A few whizzed too close over her head as she made herself a target.

She hated guns.

Then a sudden flurry of noise and shouts. A change in tone. A scream.

Of outrage.

Myra risked a look around the edge of a crate.

The woman, the sportscar man, and the gunman all stood together, backs to each other, searching the area. The sportscar man rubbed a hand over his head and looked ready to bolt. The gunman looked a little panicky, too.

The woman just looked pissed.

Like…really pissed. Like her face getting so red and her fingers so tightly clenched in a fist she might just explode from the anger.

"How did he find you?" she snarled at the gunman. But there was something in her voice… A sort of…

Hissing.

Myra blinked hard. Her stomach bottomed out.

She'd heard that sound before. That hissing beneath a growl that human voices didn't make. A combination of sounds that would be impossible for a strictly human throat to produce.

Christopher sometimes made that sound when he was angry.

She'd only ever heard that sound from dragon shifters.

But…that was impossible. There were, what, twelve dragon shifter females in the world. Only twelve. They kept to themselves, too. They were elusive. They were secretive. Most of them were supposed to be asleep.

One of them should not be standing in the middle of a warehouse in New Jersey threatening to kill a human woman over the insurance fraud committed by a Manhattan plastic surgeon.

What the hell was going on?

EIGHT

With the revelation that she might well be looking at one of the very few female dragon shifters on the planet, Myra froze for a full ten seconds. When there were shifters involved. When there was still one man holding a gun. When there was a woman's life on the line.

Ten seconds was a long time.

Ten seconds before she realized that Issa was no longer in the middle of the group trying to kill her. Ten seconds before she realized because the woman knew Christopher was here, Christopher had gotten Issa away from the people trying to kill her.

Ten seconds to realize Myra had to get the fuck out of that warehouse now.

Time for them all to escape.

She hoped Christopher had gotten Issa to safety. His need to rescue people meant he might come back for Myra, or even not leave without her, and while she admired his desire to help, she didn't want him anywhere near that female dragon shifter who looked like she wanted to explode with rage.

Myra wanted them all very far from this warehouse as soon as possible.

Ducking behind more boxes, she kept her movements as silent as possible as she hurried toward the door they'd entered through. There weren't a lot of ways out of the warehouse that weren't sealed and locked shut. And any of those options involved cracking locks and making noise—like lifting one of the docking bay doors—so she had to hope the original escape route was still clear.

The fact that it was. That nothing stepped into her way. That nothing went horribly wrong by the time she reached the exit door, forcing her to change her plans, forcing her to fall back on one of the various contingencies she'd planned out of habit, left her a little…

Uncomfortable.

Happy of course. She took the stairs two at a time and pushed out through the door, taking a hit of cold air to the face. She was delighted not to have to fall back to a backup plan.

Right?

Except…

No. No. This was fine.

She raced to the nearest building that would provide cover and hunted the skies, the surrounding roofs.

He had to be around here somewhere.

A swooping noise, the sound of rushing air. The feel of heat cutting through the cold.

She turned in time to see Christopher drop out of the sky, flying low to the tarmac in the parking lot. He wasn't carrying Issa, though.

Myra had only a moment to worry about that, to wonder about that, before he reached her and she jumped into his arms at the same instant he scooped her up.

"Issa?" she asked, watching the ground recede below her rapidly.

"Safe. For the moment. We have to get her and hurry. To my father's compound."

"That woman… She really is a…" Myra looked from the ground to Christopher's face. "She's a…"

He looked grim, his mouth a flat line, his jaw tight. Under her hands, his shoulders were tight and hard as rocks. The scales that covered his skin when his wings were out seemed more solid than usual.

Almost like armor.

"She is," he said simply.

He pumped his wings harder and they flew fast, the wind cutting sharp against Myra's face, making her eyes water. They'd flown fast to get here. She'd been with Christopher when he'd been moving very fast. But she wasn't sure she'd ever experienced flight this fast. Everything blurred around them.

She blinked. "You're cloaking?"

He hadn't cloaked much when flying with her before this. He'd cloaked after rescuing her when a wizard had nearly killed her, and he'd cloaked briefly when they'd flown into Chicago because it was another king's territory. But because it blurred their surroundings, he didn't do it much with her. She liked to see the landscape.

The fact that he was cloaking now confirmed just how serious this situation was. And how potentially deadly.

"We'll reach Issa soon," he said, ignoring her question. "I'll need to carry you both to my father's, but that will require…"

When he didn't finish, she looked at his face again, ignoring the blurring whip of Hoboken below. "Require what?"

"To carry you both safely, and reach my father's mansion fast, I need to fully shift."

Myra blinked. She'd never seen his full dragon form before. She'd seen a few others in full dragon, of course, but most dragon shifters didn't reveal themselves like that to humans. Not casually. Not just randomly. They cloaked if they had to fly in full dragon form over the city. And if they did go full dragon around humans, they often ensured it was done at a distance so it was difficult to tell just how huge they were.

They were careful not to make their true natures really obvious to humans on a regular basis because if they remained in mostly human form, humans often forgot how utterly terrifying it was to live shoulder to shoulder with beings that turned into giant fire-breathing creatures of myth.

A dragon shifter appearing full dragon to humans happened. Of course it did. It just didn't happen all the time. It was kept to rare occurrence. On purpose.

And Myra had never seen Christopher in that form.

She'd assumed, when she did, it would be… She wasn't sure. She had this idea that he'd revealed his dragon to her in some sort of formal way, in a field somewhere. Weird assumption. She'd learned a lot about dragon shifters since meeting him, but there was still a lot she didn't know, and she supposed she still harbored some strange ideas about the whole thing.

Since he'd kept his dragon form to himself this whole time, she'd just assumed revealing it was… cause for ceremony or something special or… She wasn't sure. Something anyway.

"How does that help us?" she asked trying to keep her voice even and business-like, as if this was just part of the plan and not a complete revelation. A mildly terrifying one.

An intimate one.

"I can carry you both easier in that form. My…hands are bigger. I can fly faster in that form, too."

He didn't glance behind him, but Myra did. She looked over his shoulders, past the sweep of his wings. She couldn't see the warehouse. She couldn't see anything but a blur of the landscape below.

But there was this sense of knowing. Knowing that a dragon shifter female was back there.

And she was mad.

They reached the rooftop of a multi-story apartment building near the river. At least three miles from the warehouse. He'd flown there, and back to get her, and here again, in a matter of minutes.

Issa hurried out from behind an air duct where she'd been hiding. "I can't believe you two came for me."

"We're not safe yet," Christopher said. His voice was very deep, deeper and more guttural than normal, and full of that hissing sound underneath that human vocal cords couldn't make. "We're going to the king. We'll be safe there."

"My son. She'll go after my son."

Chrisopher pulled his cellphone out of the back pocket of his jeans. He tapped in a few things on a text screen, then replaced the phone. "Your son's father and another emissary from the king will collect your son from his school. They'll meet us at the compound."

Issa closed her eyes, let out a long breath. "Thank you."

"I need to shift," he said, holding Issa's gaze. "You understand?"

She nodded. "Nothing I haven't seen before." Her smile looked forced.

Myra couldn't even force a reassuring smile. The fact that Issa had seen a dragon shifter in full dragon form wasn't technically surprising. She'd had a son with a dragon shifter. *Myra* had seen a few dragon shifters in full dragon form. At the king's mansion. In Chicago. Once or twice over the city.

She just hadn't seen *Christopher's* dragon form before.

And she kept latching on to the word "intimate" to describe the experience. Which didn't feel like it should be shared. At least this first time.

But needs must, right? This had to be done. Now. And fast.

Christopher caught her gaze. "You okay with this?"

She nodded, though the gesture felt jerky and awkward. "Hurry. We have to get out of here."

She wasn't sure how long it would take the female dragon to track them down, if she was even now currently airborne and hunting for them. No time to waste on her weird feelings. They could talk about all this when everyone was safe.

Maybe. She might not want to talk about the way she felt about this part. Maybe not ever.

Christopher narrowed his eyes at her, but then turned to look over his shoulder, in the direction of the warehouse. Even three miles away, it felt too close.

He stepped away from them, to the far end of the flat roof. There was one of the old water tanks up here still, and a lot of air vents and ducts. But enough open space on the roof, she hoped, for him to shift.

When he let his wings out, they just sort of snapped out. Appearing as if they'd been there the whole time, and he just had to unfurl them.

This was different.

A sort of swirling purple and yellow fog built up around Christopher, continued to swirl and sparkle around him, catching light, moving outward. Inside the swirl of colored fog, she saw Christopher's body convulse, heard noises that sounded like grunting. A flicker of light. More shimmering. Something that sounded like a crack. The wings along his back extended outside the fog, growing larger, longer, until they were so wide they spread the length of the roof.

The body they were attached to seemed to have grown significantly, too, though Myra couldn't see clearly through the swirling, sparkling, colored clouds. She picked up the shape of a snout. Some spikes. Definitely a lot of scale covered muscle emerging.

And then the swirling fog went higher, encompassing something much, much bigger. So big, nearly half the roof was filled by the fog obscuring the body beneath. A talon poked out of the mist, long and sharp, attached to a giant, five fingered hand covered in purple scales.

A roar came from the center of the swirling fog, a sound that reverberated across the roof and through the surroundings. She heard the screech of tires below. Knew that this transformation wasn't going unnoticed.

And then the fog swirled down, fast, collapsing back in on itself, to reveal…

The most magnificent dragon Myra had ever seen.

NINE

The dragon was easily three stories tall, even though he stood crouched on his hind legs, with a long, spike-lined tailed curling around those folded back legs. His body was thick, muscular, covered in mostly purple scales with a wash of yellow along his sides and over his stomach. The scales caught the weak winter sunlight, turning the dragon into a sparkling spot of unreality.

Myra blinked as a creature that could swallow her whole and barely notice lowered his huge head to her, bending his long neck nearly in half to get his raised snout down on her level. Though the dragon kept his mouth closed, she was acutely aware that there were a lot of teeth inside that mouth.

Turning to one side, the dragon stared at her with one eye, transparent inner lids whisked over the huge, purplish-blue iris, making it look like his eye shimmered. That faint purple glow over blue… That reminded her so sharply of Christopher she gasped.

"So," she whispered, wondering if his hearing like this was as good as when he was in his human form. "This is you as a dragon, huh?"

A small head nod and a little puff of smoke from his raised nostrils. She expected that smoke to smell vaguely of sulfur, a hint of brimstone to remind gawkers of the fire that could escape that mouth.

Except, he didn't smell like sulfur. Or even a reptile. There was a bit of Christopher there, surprisingly. But also…

"Does he smell like sugar cookies to you?" Myra asked Issa.

Issa gave her a look. A frown. Then a slow smile. "No. He doesn't. First time seeing his dragon form?"

Myra nodded, curious but too awed to ask why Issa was smiling at her. Most of her attention was still on the dragon.

A sound, in the distance, like the roar Christopher had released but louder, deeper, and distinctly more angry sounding, echoed across the buildings. Myra glanced toward that sound. Coming from the general direction of the warehouse.

That was bad.

"How do we travel this way?" she asked Christopher, panic making her less worried about the dragon in front of her who did not want to eat her because the dragon on its way just might.

He stretched out both his huge front hands. Each finger was thicker than her entire body and tipped with long, sharp talons like a ginormous hawk. Without hesitating, Issa climbed up onto one of those giant hands, and Chrisopher gently closed his dragon fingers around the woman, cradling her in his grip as she wrapped her arms around the digit that looked most like a thumb.

Myra looked at the hand stretched out to her. Then the eye focused on her. The little wink of the inner lids. Okay. So. He intended on carrying them this way. Took that whole saying of having someone in the palm of your hand a little literally, but she could do this.

Her heartbeat pounding, the rush of fear sent a spike of adrenaline into her blood. And the charge sent another bolt of excitement hot on its heels. The fear and excitement left her a little giddy. The knowledge that Christopher wouldn't drop her tipped the balance toward excitement and she scrambled into his palm. Her eyes widened as the huge fingers closed in around her, gently, giving her a comfortable cage to ride in. She did as Issa had done and hugged her arms as best she could around his thumb.

Beating wings that could knock over a building if he wasn't careful, the dragon launched into the sky. More cars screeching below. A few shouts. Then that blurring around them. And with a pump of his wings, they streaked across the sky. Out over the river before she could blink. High enough to see the island of Manhattan below. So high, the air was sharp and a little hard to breathe. Her ears popped as he dropped again a moment later, spiraling downward at such dizzying speed, even Myra had a moment of vertigo.

She gripped his thumb tighter and leaned out enough to see the ground rising up to them fast. To see the king's compound already beneath them. Wow. That had taken less than two minutes. Like he'd stretched his length and they were already here.

The sound of Issa's squeal reminded Myra that she should probably be afraid of the rapid decent. They were coming in fast and hard and the landing roof on the top of the king's mansion was approaching so rapidly it took up most of her vision.

But this was Christopher, even in this terrifying form. And in her soul, she knew he'd keep her from hitting the ground.

He swung upward at the last minute, giving his huge wings a strong beat, and settled onto his hind legs on the open landing area on the roof as lightly as if he'd just floated down.

The multiple and sudden changes in both speed and altitude left Myra both dizzy and a little nauseated. She liked a good roller coaster as much as the next girl, but that one had been a bit much.

Still, they were at the compound now, and there were other dragons here. And the king. That female dragon would have to go through a lot of other dragons to get to them. The nausea and disorientation were worth the distance they'd put between themselves and the female.

Christopher set his taloned hands down on the red sandstone roof, opening his fingers so Myra and Issa could scramble off his palms. Behind him, there were already about a dozen men hurrying up onto the roof. Dragons didn't drop in on the king unannounced. Certainly not at the speed Christopher had.

But they all must have recognized his dragon because no one had tried to shoot him out of the sky with whatever weapon they had in the two guard towers flanking the mansion. Something to do with fire. She knew enough to know she didn't want personal experience with those weapons.

Instead of firing on him, the twelve men formed up in a wide circle around Christopher, like a guard, and waited.

She recognized some of them as people she'd seen around the mansion on her few visits here. But she hadn't been introduced to any of them so didn't have names.

The swirl of purple-yellow smoke that had accompanied Christopher's shift to his dragon swirled around him again. Both Myra and Issa stepped away, all the way to the line of the circling guards. The swirl hid most of the shift, a reverse process of what had happened on the apartment roof in Hoboken. Large taloned hands shrank into the fog, tail and wings compressed so they were no longer visible, the fog itself shrank, and shrank some more.

When everything settled, the sparkling fog vanishing in a whisp, Christopher stood in the middle of a wide open space on the roof, wearing basically what he'd had on before. His jeans. No shoes now. No shirt. His dark hair mussed. His blue eyes still holding a faint glow of purplish gold.

He wasn't even breathing hard.

And for some reason, she still smelled sugar cookies.

She was going to have to ask about the sugar cookies. He didn't always have that added element to his scent. Just occasionally. Mostly he just smelled like the soap he used and that faint leathery-reptilian underscent of his dragon. There were hints of vanilla all the time, but the smell of actual *cookies* was so strong in that moment, she started to crave cookies.

This was not the time for cookies!

Christopher strode over to them, his brows lowered, giving him a fierce, almost mean look. The scowl bracketing his mouth tight. Issa pulled in a sharp breath and took a step backward.

Myra gave her a look. She'd been okay climbing up into his hand when he'd been gigantic and could breathe fire, but his scowl made her nervous? Weird.

Myra noticed the guards were also straightening and their gazes darted away from Christopher. She just couldn't see how everyone was so intimidated by a man who currently smelled like sugar and vanilla.

She looked back at him. To be fair, the scowl was pretty ferocious. He was not a happy dragon.

"We need to get inside," she said, stepping

close to him. "Get Issa away." She lowered her voice. "Her son?"

Christopher glanced at one of the guards.

The guard snapped even straighter, if that was possible, and said, "Arrived moments before you, Highness. They're inside."

Myra heard Issa's sob and turned in time to catch the woman before her legs collapsed out from under her. "Yeah, we need to get her inside."

At a brief nod from Christopher, the guards formed up tighter around him, Myra, and Issa and escorted them all inside.

The roof was an open space, half grass for the younglings to land on, half red sandstone, circled by a low wall decorated with dragon statues. Under normal circumstances, it was a pretty space, giving great views of the surrounding woods and, in one direction, the high spears and lights of Manhattan far below.

But with the threat of an angry female dragon looming, Myra was just as happy to get off the roof.

The entrance to the castle from the roof was through a low ceiling ramp that could be closed off with titanium doors infused with fire-resistant magic. You wanted to defend against dragons, you had to use fire and defend against it.

For the most part, though, dragon shifters

fighting dragon shifters hadn't been an issue in Myra's lifetime. She was glad the king had built this place with that possibility in mind, though.

The door rolled down behind them as soon as they were all inside, sealing off the roof entrance. The lights inside came on in a flicker of brightness and then…

"Mommy!"

A tiny whirlwind zipped past Myra and right into Issa's arms. Issa caught the whirlwind with only a single grunt and then a lot of tears and petting dark hair and kissing little cheeks.

The boy looked about seven or eight in human years, but Christopher had said he was only five so maybe he was just big for his age. Myra wasn't much of a judge for kid ages, though. It was good to know what a proper youngling looked like. She realized as she watched the mother and son reunion, this was the first time she'd seen a dragon shifter kid who she knew for sure was a dragon shifter.

Another man strode through the guards and up to Issa and the boy. He was tall, a reasonable sort of tall. Just over six foot. Not as huge as Christopher. Thickly muscled, light blond hair, brown eyes, skin a few shades browner than Issa's. Myra spotted a tattoo along the back of his neck, but she couldn't see the details.

As far as she was aware, shifters lost their tattoos every time they changed shape, so to keep one meant regularly reapplying the tattoo. Lot of time in a chair with needles for body art. She admired the commitment.

"You okay?" the man asked Issa quietly, setting a gentle hand to her back, sort of hugging both Issa and the boy.

"Fine. Fine now. The prince and Myra saved me."

Myra appreciated being given a name in that exchange and not just referred to as "the thief."

The man looked at her and Christopher, bowing his head a little and dropping his gaze to the ground. "Thank you," he said.

Christopher nodded sharply. "Please take Issa to the rooms prepared. You can all rest there."

The man nodded, and Issa, her son, and the man who was obviously the boy's father walked through the circling guard and disappeared around a corner in the mansion.

That Christopher knew there'd be a room ready for the small family spoke well of the mansion staff's efficiency.

"Any signs of the female?" Christopher asked one of the trailing guards as the rest of them turned down a different corridor, heading toward the throne room and the no-doubt waiting king.

"Nothing on radar yet. We've warned air traffic control towers in the area."

"Good thinking," Christopher muttered.

Yeah, Myra thought, last thing they needed was a giant female dragon knocking commercial airliners out of the sky.

She'd read that female dragon shifters were huge, but after seeing Christopher up close and personal, she wondered just how big a female really was. Since they were a lot larger than the males, and Christopher was the size he was in dragon form, that meant the female could be as large as the entire island of Manhattan. And that was utterly terrifying.

"You ever encountered a female dragon before," she murmured to Christopher as they stalked through the corridors. The guard around them peeled off as they went, she presumed to take up defensive positions.

"Not in person," he said.

"Why didn't she...smell you in the warehouse?" Dragons had a good sense of smell. They weren't like werewolves or some of the cat shifters, but their sense of smell was still significantly better than a human's. Christopher and the female should have been able to at least smell each other, right?

"That's complicated." He gave her a sideways

look. "There are some things about dragon shifters that aren't…public knowledge."

"Not public knowledge?"

"You'd have to be part of a dragon shifter community to know."

"I see. Is this something you can't tell me?"

"No. It's not that. It's…complicated."

A wash of red swept up his pale cheeks, a blush that for the life of her Myra couldn't understand.

"Later," he promised. "After we deal with the current crisis."

Her curiosity was bursting for answers. But she pressed her lips together to keep them in. He was right.

They had a crisis to deal with first.

TEN

The few times Myra had been inside the throne room, the place had either been empty or a handful of dragon shifters had filled it. It was a huge, high ceiling room with the king's actual throne—a big piece of gold and bone furniture encrusted with precious jewels she hadn't figured out how to steal yet—on a dais across from the giant wooden doors that led into the room.

This day, there were at least a dozen men moving through the room, a sort of controlled chaos of passing around information, working on tablets and phones, everyone seeming to talk at once. There was a table against one wall that hadn't been there before, set up with computers and what looked like a radar system. There was beeping, and shouting, and talking, and so much noise it echoed off the high ceilings.

But it all seemed controlled. The shouting was just to be heard above the din. The rapid-fire conversations intense and focused. The movements around the table and back and forth to the king or out the door calculated and well-choreographed so no one bumped into anyone else.

The king stood to one side of the room, looking at documents put into his hands, or studying something on a tablet held up for him occasionally. His throne was empty, and while she knew it wasn't the time, Myra did indulge in one longing glance at all those imbedded precious stones currently going unnoticed by anyone else in the room.

Christopher hooked a hand through her elbow, which made her wonder if he'd realized where her mind had momentarily strayed, and hurried up to his father. The king currently had his head tilted toward another man who was nearly as tall as Christopher and bore a remarkable resemblance to the king. Dark hair, light eyes, pale skin, a certain cut to his jaw and nose.

Myra's gaze jumped between the man with the king and Christopher. Yeah. There in the mouth.

The nose. This must be one of Christopher's brothers.

He had a bunch, apparently, but no one knew quite how many sons the king had, or what they all looked like. Some were known by name in the gossip columns, like Christopher had once been. But even those didn't apparently encompass all the king's offspring. As the king had said on that first day he'd commanded her to go rescue Christopher, there were no pictures of the royal family allowed. Many people knew the king on sight. He was hard to miss and he usually ensured those who saw him knew he was the king. People talked about his looks even if there were no pictures. But the appearances of most of the sons were still illusive and vague.

Coming face-to-face with one of Christopher's brothers sent another bolt of curiosity through her. Shame they had the female dragon to worry about. She had a lot of questions she couldn't ask yet.

Christopher paused at the radar screen, watching the small glowing green dot on the darker green background. There were other, smaller dots on the screen, all moving away from the larger dot.

"All planes in the area are landing or diverting to other airports, Highness," the man sitting in front of the radar screen told Christopher.

"Good. Is she on her way?"

"She's remained in this spot—" the man gestured to the singular dot, "—the entire time I've been monitoring her. We're not sure what she's doing."

Christopher gave a brief nod, then moved to join his father and—probably?—his brother.

"Tell me," the king said without preamble.

Christopher went over everything that had happened that day, their meeting with Issa at the café—the king cast Myra an unreadable look at that—Issa's kidnapping by the two gunmen from the coffee shop, the chase, the New Jersey warehouse, the sportscar man, and finally the woman.

The king nodded as he listened, his mouth pursed. He snarled at Christopher's description of the woman. His eyes narrowed and, somewhat surprisingly, he cursed under his breath.

She'd witnessed the king angry. Witnessed him pretending to be angry. Seen him barely controlling that anger.

She'd never seen him…nervous.

"That would be Jasmin," he said after a moment. "One of the younger females."

Which, given females lived millennia, could still mean she was thousands of years old.

"Young" for a female dragon was relative, so Myra had learned.

"What's all this have to do with a plastic surgeon and insurance fraud?" Myra asked into the silence following the revelation of the female dragon's name.

The king's gaze flicked to her. "Jasmin gathers wealth the way we all do, but she prefers to do it in ways that…give her a charge."

"Illegal stuff," Myra said, shrugging. She got that. She was a thief after all. Though, she didn't really do it for the money anymore. She did it for the fun and the challenge. And the adrenaline rush.

"Illegal," the king murmured. "But more than that. She takes human partners. Manipulates them. Kills them when she's tired of them or they get in her way. Bodies build up around Jasmin when she's working a con." Another unreadable expression crossed the king's features. "All this might be forgiven in another era, but in modern times, given our treaties with the humans, this can be…awkward. She keeps a low profile most of the time. And usually doesn't tangle with other dragons as part of her schemes."

"Maybe she didn't realize anyone at the plastic surgeon's practice had ties to the dragons here."

Issa *was* human after all. "At least not when she started her con."

Because Jasmin had absolutely known Issa's son was a dragon by the time they got to that warehouse.

"Incoming," the man at the radar shouted, and everyone in the room stilled.

The silence that fell rang in Myra's ears. People never really thought about it if silence wasn't part of their profession, but *silence* had both weight and sound to it. Sometimes the sound of a space's silence was hard to describe. At that moment, Myra had no trouble describing the silence that had just fallen over the throne room.

It was the silence of collective dread.

The king exchanged a look with the son he hadn't introduced yet. Then with Christopher. All three men looked grim.

Myra glanced between them and the radar screen which had started beeping. The beeping increased. The sound was loud in the quiet room.

Myra wanted to do something, but most of her instincts were the run-and-hide sort. She was a field mouse to this circling hawk, and she very much wanted to go to ground and get very still and wait for the hawk to fly over, hoping it didn't see her.

Except the dragon already knew who she was,

and where she was, and there was no hiding from this.

Probably a good thing she was a mouse with a lot of smaller hawk friends. Still. What could even an entire dragon cohort do against one angry female dragon.

Nowhere in anything she'd ever researched had she learned how a female dragon could be killed. The males could be killed. They lived centuries and were incredibly *hard* to kill. But it could be done. Nothing she'd read, that was publicly available, had hinted at a way to kill a female dragon.

Was it even possible?

And, given there were only twelve in the world, was it…right? Jasmin didn't sound like a nice person. Actually, she sounded like a serial killer to Myra, though it was hard to judge dragons by human standards. But she was one of twelve. One of so very few living female dragons. Even if they could kill her, *should* they try?

Would Jasmin even give the cohort a choice?

The beeping had gotten so loud, so persistent, Myra could practically feel the presence of the dragon overhead. Circling the compound, a shadow over the city. Her heartbeat seemed to have sped up with the beeping too, until it was pounding so hard in her chest it almost hurt. She liked a good adrenaline rush and that touch of fear as much as the next person, but this was too much, even for her.

"What do we do?" she finally blurted out into the tense silence.

The man who the king hadn't introduced yet, who might well be another one of his son's, said, "We negotiate with her and hope she leaves."

Myra looked toward the radar screen and the incessant beeping. "That doesn't sound…"

"Likely," Christopher finished for her.

"And what would you have us do?" the possible brother asked Christopher. "We can't remain locked down inside the mansion forever. There are innocent humans in the city we have to worry about if she gets very angry."

"She doesn't want to bring the human world down on her," Christopher said, sounding very reasonable. Myra latched onto that reasonable tone of voice to calm her fears. "Having human militaries from around the world hunting her will never suit. She won't be able to rest. And if she destroys this world, or rallies the other females to try, it will leave her with no games to play." Christopher shrugged. "There's also the very real likelihood one of the other females will not take kindly to the way Jasmin courts disaster."

Oh. Wow. The thought of another female

dragon fighting with Jasmin seemed like it might not go well for all the unfortunate human settlements below them.

"Then we negotiate," the possible brother said with a firm nod.

"Negotiate what?" Christopher said.

"We turn over the human she wants," the brother said.

"No," Christopher and Myra said at the same time.

Where Christopher had that hissing growl in his voice, Myra's sounded almost like a snarl. Given the circumstances, she was surprised she could snarl at a dragon shifter who stood easily a foot taller than her and was twice as wide and could snap her like a twig. But given what was circling overhead, the possible brother seemed like less of a threat.

That was saying something.

"We negotiate," the king said, his voice firm. "We turn over no one as sacrifice." He glanced at Christopher. "The time of feeding virgins to dragons is done."

Myra was glad to hear that. Not that she was a virgin. Nor was Issa for that matter. But still, she appreciated the confirmation.

"What do you intend on offering her, then,

father?" the now confirmed, but still unnamed son asked.

The king's gaze dropped to Myra, and Christopher immediately stepped in front of her.

"I said we turn over no sacrifices," the king growled, his eyes narrowing at his son.

"Myra has done enough," Christopher said. "She's not part of this."

"Jasmin knows of her. She is now."

And didn't that just suck.

"Jasmin gathers a not insignificant amount of her wealth in a hoard in New Jersey," the king said. "If she knew that hoard was vulnerable, she would be willing to negotiate a…compromise."

Myra noticed he didn't say a peace. She had a feeling Jasmin didn't do "peace."

"Where's this hoard and how hard is it to break into?" Myra asked. She knew a job offer when she heard one. "Also, I do this for you? This is absolutely the last job. Got it?"

The unnamed son frowned and looked between her and the king. Christopher remained standing in front of her, but he didn't speak up or try to prevent her from considering the king's suggestion.

"Her hoard is…not as difficult as mine was to access. She's a female. No one would dare try for her hoard. Not even master thieves."

Myra's mouth twitched with a smile she refused to release. And no, she wasn't preening or delighted by the king calling her a master thief. This was not a preening situation. It wouldn't do for the king to know he could compliment her into taking one of his jobs either. Bad enough he knew her soft spot for a challenge.

"Also, the location of her hoard is not generally known, whereas mine…is."

"But you know where she keeps her hoard," Myra said.

"This part of it anyway. It is not her only collection. But any of them being vulnerable will…give her pause."

"Pause long enough for the rest of us to grow old and die before she decides to start making trouble again?"

"Long enough for her to not lay siege to Manhattan for another century."

That sounded good. Myra was likely to be dead by the time that century passed. Jasmin would be someone else's problem then.

She cut off any thought of where Christopher would be in a century. That was a long time off and they had more than enough to think about right now.

"Okay." Myra straightened her shoulders. She could do this. If this would get Jasmin to go away and leave everyone, including Issa, alone, then she could do this. This was even better motivation than a bet. And she'd only sworn off breaking into a dragon *king's* hoard. She'd never promised herself she'd stay out of *all* dragon hoards. "Where am I going? Specifically."

"I'm going with you," Christopher said, quietly. But his voice carried through the mostly silent throne room.

Except for the beeping that indicated a terrifying female dragon was circling overhead and the conversation the king, his two sons, and Myra were having, the rest of the throne room remained silent. Watching. Listening.

Waiting.

ELEVEN

Getting to the wooded area not far from Trenton without being seen sneaking out of the king's compound by the female dragon circling overhead had proved less complicated than Myra had feared. The king went out onto the roof to negotiate with Jasmin. Jasmin had landed and shifted.

And the minute she was in human form instead of dragon form, Myra and Christopher had taken flight from a position much farther down the hill. An exit that, ironically, was only accessible through the king's hoard.

Christopher watched her closely as they went through, which, if she were being honest, was a little insulting. Yes, yes, all the piles of sparkly shinys were a bit distracting. But not when the potential for all of Manhattan to be laid waste by an angry female dragon was on the line.

Christopher had cloaked and then flown at that speed she hadn't realized was possible until the escape from Jasmin. A speed that blurred the surroundings and made her cling tight to his neck as much for the warmth of his body as the worry about just how fast they were going. She couldn't even really enjoy the adrenaline rush, the speed of it all, because she was too aware of what she'd left back at the king's mansion.

The hoard was in an underground compound, accessed by a single door hidden in the woods, at a specific set of coordinates the king had given Christopher and which he seemed able to pinpoint without GPS, which was pretty impressive. But the location was surrounded by tightly packed trees and difficult to get to by flight. Christopher couldn't just land next to the door without risking the delicate membranes stretched between bone on his wings. He had to find a clearing, and they had to hike in to the door.

Door was maybe a little grand for the entrance. More like a secured metal cover over a hole, similar to a manhole cover, only bigger. Roughly four feet in diameter. If there wasn't some sort of hydraulic mechanism that lifted that big slab of copper, she'd have had a hard time lifting it out of the way without Christopher.

The copper plated disk wasn't just locked either. The minute Myra hovered her hand over the thing, she felt the crinkling static of magic. Lots of magic. More than the typical dragon usually had around their things.

"Do female dragons do magic?" she murmured as she explored the spells with her eyes closed, teasing out the base of them so she could find a way to crack them.

"Not like wizards. Or even you. Not spells."

"She hired someone to do this, then," Myra said. "Because this is thief magic." Not wizard magic. This magic had the…flavor, she supposed. The flavor of her own special brand of power. And it was old. These spells had been here for a while.

"Can you break them?" Christopher sounded worried.

"So little faith," she muttered as she dug through the spells, looking for the key to the lock and… Ah. There it was. Tricky tricky, former thief whoever they were.

It took a bit of finessing and a lot more of her own magic than she usually had to use. Picking at the spells and teasing them far enough apart to insert the metaphorical magic key took her a good ten minutes. Much longer than she would have liked. But to rush this would have set off an alarm. An alarm she was certain Jasmin would know about instantly.

The king was giving her time by negotiating with Jasmin. If Myra tipped her hand too soon, the entire plan was ruined and the king might end up dead before Myra even knew she'd fucked up.

Thinking about the consequences usually screwed up her concentration, so she kept her focus on the magical tangle and when she finally broke through the spells, the mental *click* was supremely satisfying.

She eased back onto her haunches and pressed the center of the disk. It hissed open, lifting about an inch before stopping.

"You're up," she said to Christopher. "You can safely lift it off and set it aside now. Please and thank you."

That last earned her a small smile.

Christopher lifted the heavy disk like it weighed a few pounds instead of probably closer to several hundred pounds, and Myra tried not to admire his muscles as he did because, again, not the moment.

The opening beneath the disk revealed a long, round tunnel and ladder which went so deep into the ground, the darkness closed in like a fist, the sunny winter afternoon light barely reaching four feet into the concrete pipe. She pulled a glow stick from one of her vest pockets and cracked it, letting it drop into the tunnel.

It went a long way down.

The sound of it hitting the ground was also very faint.

Along the way, it lit up the narrow pipe and ladder. She'd be able to slip down the tunnel easily enough, but it was going to be tight for Christopher. She supposed that was on purpose, as only another dragon was likely to want to break into a dragon's hoard. Humans were not typically that suicidal.

She wasn't either. Just...more motivated by challenge than the next human.

Glancing back at Christopher, she confirmed he'd shifted his wings away. Then pulled out another glow stick and broke it, looping it through a cloth tab in her vest so she had her hands free to climb down the ladder.

"I'll go first," Christopher said. "In case there are traps below."

"What if they're magical traps? Probably specifically designed for dragons since this whole set up seems designed to keep dragons out?"

His jaw worked as he looked over her shoulder into the concrete pipe. They couldn't see the glow stick below anymore. She'd barely been able to see it before hearing the *chink chink* sound of it hitting the ground. She considered that Christopher might be able to still see it. Or he could see in the dark well enough, he had a good view down the tunnel. Her night vision was excellent, a part of the magic that made her such an excellent thief, but her vision didn't compare to a shapeshifter's.

"You can guard me from above, if someone tries to follow us down the tunnel," she said, by way of mollifying his need to protect. "Will that help? Make you feel better?"

"No. But you can go first." He tilted his head to one side, then the other, as if loosening muscles in his neck. "There's no way for me to open wings in that pipe."

"I know. On purpose. We'll be okay."

She rose up and gave him a very solid, very firm kiss right on the mouth. A move that startled him enough he didn't react immediately. Then he pulled her into a tight grip, his hands on her waist, bringing her up on her toes. The height difference between them was sometimes ridiculous, but she loved it. The power, the strength so casually displayed, the desperation just under his kiss all made her blood sing.

She pulled back as quickly as she'd jumped in. But now her skin tingled. Her body buzzed with energy. And the fear coiling in her gut tipped toward excitement.

"We've got this." She grinned and patted his bare chest. "It'll be fun."

He didn't smile back. His hands flexed in her vest, tightening around her convulsively, before he let her go.

She slid down onto the ladder, tempted to just slide down the rails to the ground because it was so far below, but she worried about traps along the way, so a slow descent it was.

Relatively slow. They only had so much time.

As much time as the king could manage to stall an angry female dragon.

Before she decided to just light the world on fire.

TWELVE

The darkness closed around Myra, leaving a tiny halo of fading sunlight above which was mostly blocked by Christopher as he moved down into the tunnel. The green light from the glow stick fastened to her vest provided a bubble of illumination, enough for her to ensure her grip and footing on the ladder, enough she could search for traps in her immediate area. But she couldn't see very far below her feet.

Myra was comfortable in the dark. She loved the dark. It hid all sorts of comings and goings and made her job infinitely easier. She *lived* in the dark.

But this was a different kind of dark. She'd heard this kind of dark, the blackness that had weight to it, called stygian darkness. That word had never felt more appropriate than it did just then.

She was *aware* of the earth beyond the concrete pipe that cut through the soil. She was aware of the weight of that earth closing in around them. A little too aware that this tube with its narrow circumference and thin ladder had been built by a dragon shifter determined to protect the wealth buried beneath. The entire thing could be a trap, seal off, burying her and Christopher alive.

Myra hadn't ever really thought about being buried alive. Her jobs had never taken her into places that gave that impression. Even the king's hoard, buried as it was beneath his mansion into the rocky foundation of the hills on which the compound sat, hadn't given her this feeling.

There had been something…open about getting to the king's hoard. A sense that she could get back out again.

This space felt like it was swallowing her. The darkness devouring and dissolving her until she would cease to exist.

The feeling was so strong she started hunting for illusion spells and panic spells on the ladder.

"You feeling this?" she murmured up to Christopher. "A kind of panic as we go deeper?"

He grunted, a sound which could mean anything but she interpreted it as a yes.

If he was feeling this dread, though, it probably meant magic. But she couldn't feel anything in the ladder. She would have picked that up immediately.

Spells like this needed an anchor. She called up a warning to Christopher and then paused to set her fingers against the pipe's wall.

Well shit. "Spell in the concrete. All of it. The entire pipe is bespelled."

"We should get out."

"It's a panic spell. Designed to drive us back up. Only way out now is through. So to speak." She let her own magic drift through the puzzle of the spell on the walls. "Yeah, I can't break this. It's too extensive. But it's not dangerous. Technically. It's just designed to fuck with your thinking. So just… Ignore your own thoughts until after we reach the bottom."

"My own thoughts are telling me what we'll find at the bottom will be worse than this spell."

"Exactly what they would be telling you under the influence of this spell." She started back down the ladder.

Ignoring panic and fear and the sense of being destroyed the farther down the tunnel she went was not as easy as she'd made it sound. The feeling grabbed onto her lizard brain, triggering her flight instincts so strongly she had to clamp her lips tightly together to keep from shouting up at Christopher to climb out of the tunnel again.

She physically had to force herself not to scramble back up the ladder. Force herself, rung by rung, to keep moving downward.

Given the level of wealth and treasure beneath her, the desire to run away was so contrary to her natural instincts, it was amazing. That contrast, that disconnect from how she'd usually face these sorts of situations, allowed her to keep moving when the panic pushed her so hard it made breathing difficult.

They reached the ground suddenly, the light from her previous glow stick having winked out already. Not even a faint glow, which was weird. Like the darkness ate light.

She realized the glow stick in her vest was fading fast too and quickly cracked another one. She only had a few more after this, so she had to hope whatever was eating the light down here— probably the dread spells worked into the pipe walls—still gave her enough time to get them back out again.

The pipe ended in a dirt floor and…nothing else. No obvious doors or exits or passages into the other parts of the hoard. She knew this wasn't the end of it. If she hadn't had the kind of magic she had, she might have been fooled. Might have thought she'd forced her way through all that horrible fear and panic for nothing.

But her fingertips were tingling and anticipation hummed in her gut. There was treasure here somewhere. Nearby. Close enough she could practically smell it. And she didn't have a shifter's sense of smell.

"Dead end?" Christopher asked, sounding appalled.

He was still on the ladder because there wasn't enough room at the bottom of the pipe for them to both stand on the ground without being wrapped around each other. While that sounded delightful in a different setting, she needed room to study the walls and ground.

"There's something here," she murmured. "I can feel it. Just have to find it."

She studied the walls, squatted to run her fingers over the dirt floor. As she neared one particular part of the floor, at the joint where the ground met the pipe, she felt an increase in the dread and panic. A punch to her lizard brain that robbed her of breath. It was like getting hit with a shock of electricity, but electricity made of panic that wrapped around her most primitive instincts.

She grinned. There it was.

Running her fingers over the spot, ignoring the churning in her gut and the way her body hair raised, she dug around until she found the metal ring. Like a thick chainlink, imbedded into the dirt. She tugged it up and into view, dirt drifting around it and throwing up the scent of dry mustiness and sand. A quick study confirmed a small locking spell on the link. Nothing complicated. Just a lock that made pulling up the full chain impossible.

She only needed thirty seconds to crack the spell, though she had to wave Christopher to silence once before he broke her concentration. Once she had the spell cracked, she grinned up at him and tugged hard on the link. A chain rose up out of the ground.

And a crack appeared at the base of one section of the pipe.

"Here, you pull this. You're the one with the muscles."

He raised a sardonic eyebrow at her, which she could only just see in the fading green light. She was tempted to crack another glow stick, but they were so close to getting out of the pipe, she resisted. They might need those sticks later.

As Christopher pulled on the chain, dragging it up through the dirt like a magic trick, the tiny bit of space that had appeared grew, raising an entire section of the concrete pipe until a person-sized doorway appeared.

Beyond that doorway was more darkness. But Myra's fingertips were tingling hard now. Treasure. Close.

She tried not to giggle because, really, this wasn't her normal sort of heist. But still. She was breaking into another hoard. And there was something so *satisfying* in that accomplishment.

Christopher stopped her walking through the black hole in the tunnel with an arm across her chest. She looked up at him with a raised brow.

"Breaking in is the point," he said. "We aren't here to empty her hoard. Just get one thing to prove we've been here."

"Same as when I broke into your father's hoard," she said with a shrug. "I realize making an enemy of a female dragon is a bad idea."

Even though it was already too late. She'd already made an enemy. One she really didn't want. But the job was done. This was just the icing on the hate cake.

"This is to make a point," Christopher reiterated. "One that will force Jasmin to back off. We hope. So we don't take anything too valuable that she'll miss."

"I get it," she told him. "I do. Don't worry. I know what I'm doing."

The difference here was that Jasmin didn't have a cohort of fellow dragons to capture Myra in the act. Female dragons were loners, independent, kept to themselves. There was no cohort. And Christopher could take care of any unlucky humans Jasmin might have hired to live down here and guard her hoard.

Even that seemed unlikely, though. Dragons did *not* like anyone inside their hoards. Even guards.

Christopher held her gaze for a beat, then nodded and finally dropped off the ladder, landing lightly on the dirt floor next to her. They were still inside the pipe so they were pressed tight together. The feel of his heat enveloping her was exactly as delicious as she'd expected. Also a little distracting.

Still, she leaned into him, and he set his hands to her shoulders, holding her close for a moment as they both contemplated the black hole opening before them.

"More traps?" he murmured against her hair.

"Probably. But not on the doorway." On the other side... She'd have to go through the doorway to see.

"Can I at least go first this time?"

"Nope." She had to go first to look out for

spells still. "You guard our backs, big guy. I've got our fronts. We've got this."

She felt his chest expand and contract behind her with his deep breath. The release of that breath ruffled the top of her hair. The bun she'd wrapped her hair into had loosened enough over the course of the day for fine strands to stick to her temples. The air at this depth should have been cold, freezing even. And it was chilled. But not as cold as it should have been. And between that and Christopher's heat at her back, Myra felt sweat start to trickle down her cheeks.

She gave in to the need to see, cracked a third glow stick, and held it in front of her as they moved through the black doorway. Christopher kept his hands on her shoulders, ready to pull her away from danger. She tried not to think about the danger, to concentrate on the treasure ahead that she could *feel*.

But she was very grateful she had Christopher at her back.

THIRTEEN

A short, dark, metal tunnel that Christopher had to duck to walk through closed in around them as they passed through the black doorway. Myra wasn't claustrophobic, but the tightness of the space made her very aware of all the earth above. She wasn't sure if that awareness was part of the magical panic she'd felt coming down the ladder or if this was just common sense and survival instincts, but she was glad the tunnel was short this time.

It opened out onto a larger room, with enough space for Christopher to finally stand his full height. The room was just a giant steel box. Without much to recommend it. A dry, dusty smell, so no mold which was good. And a low level of heat seemed to emanate from the walls.

Not enough to make her sweat, though she was doing that thanks to Christopher's heat at her back, but enough to keep the room from being as chilled as an underground bunker should have been.

"That heat a spell?" she asked, moving closer to one of the walls to hold her hand in front of it. Definitely warmer than buried metal should be. "Not, like, deadly radiation or anything, right?"

The tingle of a spell along her palm helped assure her this was magic. Still, she glanced back at Christopher with her brows raised in question.

"Not radiation," he said. "That would kill Jasmine eventually, too."

Interesting to learn something would kill a female dragon. Even if it did take a while. "Only if she spent enough time down here."

"This is part of her hoard. She spends time here."

That peaked Myra's curiosity. "Do you hang out in your hoard a lot?"

"There doesn't seem to be a hoard of anything here," he said, avoiding her question. She suspected if the light hadn't been green from her glow stick, she might have seen him blush.

"There's another door around here," she said. "This would be an antechamber. Like in mummy tombs and stuff."

"How do you know that?"

"I know treasure rooms," she said. She'd been in a few in her time. "Your father has a nice antechamber for his hoard. Designed to look like you've found the hoard with lots of valuables in it. Pretty clever actually. If a thief didn't know better. Lot of traps in that room."

She glanced at Christopher long enough to see his mouth twitch, but he schooled his features before she could tell if he was about to grin or scowl. Shame. She could have used his grin at that moment. Scowl could have been nice, too. He looked sexy either way.

She continued walking the perimeter of the room, her hand out to her side, hovering just in front of the wall without touching it. The tingles of magic were pleasant, like the feel of the warmth from the wall. Nothing stinging or irritating or sending out little electrical shocks. Or even the dread she'd felt in the vertical pipe.

"Glad it's not lighting up my lizard brain anymore," she muttered.

"That was…uncomfortable."

She snort-laughed. "Understatement. Ah. Here we go." She ran her hand above an area of wall that definitely felt different. Less heat. Less magic tingling over her palm. No, not less. Different.

There was a different magic here. Not dread or warning, though.

"The lock." She wagged her eyebrows at Christopher.

She was probably having too much fun, given what was at stake. But being on the scent of treasure, now that she had a lock to crack, with untold riches just the other side of the door, the thrill of the hunt thrummed in her blood. She'd felt similarly cracking the lock on the copper disk covering the tunnel up in the woods. But now she *knew* she was close. *Knew* the hoard was just beyond this wall.

Only one more trap. One more lock. The king was right. This wasn't as hard as breaking into his hoard had been. Not easy. But not hard. For someone like her.

Christopher walked up behind her as she had her eyes half closed, working her way through this last trap.

Quietly, most of her attention on the bespelled lock, she said, "Jasmin depended on the dread spell worked into the concrete of the vertical pipe. I can see why. Most people wouldn't have been motivated to work their way through that even with the treasure at the other end."

"Would you? If you didn't have your current

motivation of preventing Manhattan from burning?"

She shrugged. "Maybe. Oh. There we go."

She felt the little snick as she hit the spot in the trap that released the pressure and let the spell dissipate. She wasn't entirely sure what would have happened if she'd triggered the spell rather than broken it. Probably killed her. But she thought better of mentioning that out loud.

One more check. Nothing in the way. She set her hand to the pressure plate in the wall and pushed. A lot of clicking and whirring and noise echoed around the room. The entire room.

She stepped away from the wall, to the center of the square space. She'd been expecting a door to open, like an ordinary door. Instead, the room all around them creaked and hitched and slid. Metal over metal. Churning clink of metal chains and things spinning.

The room folded back on itself, starting from the ceiling, folding open, then down the walls, the room disappearing panel by panel until it had folded completely into the floor.

Myra blinked. "Huh."

She held up her glow stick. The light broke through the darkness now surrounding them, but not very far. Only enough to reveal the room they now stood in was immense, rising up high above them and spreading out around them.

They'd been led into the center of a chamber, into a box that had been *inside* the huge, cavernous room. And with that box gone…

The hoard spread out around them.

Her glow stick only revealed the edges of it. The piles and piles of…sparkling stuff. Myra sighed and her heart beat harder. So many sparkly things. Even the edges of the treasure awed her. Made her yearn.

She loved treasure.

"Beautiful," she whispered. And even her whisper echoed.

"Are you going to cry?" Christopher asked.

"Maybe."

She eased forward, to the closest pile of stuff. Gold goblets, and boxes, and bars of gold all draped with gold chains and coins. And in the middle of all that gold, multi-colored precious and semi-precious stones winked in a rainbow. And where there were clear diamonds, they caught the green light of her glow stick and made strange prisms.

"We need something that will assure Jasmin we've been to her hoard and not just picked up something from another hoard," Christopher said.

"I suppose that would have been an option for

someone who has a hoard." She glanced back at him, eyebrows raised.

He didn't rise to the bait this time either. "That necklace. The one with the diamond medallion on it. That's old. Older than the things surrounding it. That would do."

She nodded, shrugged. But she'd spotted something she thought might work better. "How about this?"

Lifting the little cut diamond dragon from the middle of all that gold, she held it up to her glow stick. Green light skittered over the cuts in the miniature statue. The dragon was exquisite. Each angle and curve intricately detailed. All the detail turned the diamond dragon into repeating prisms of light inside light. The dragon was sitting on its hind legs, its tail wrapped around its feet, like a cat. Wings open and angled backward, but not spread out to the side. Thick body, long neck, head arched down so the dragon looked like it was looking at something near its feet.

"There's another statue that goes with this one," Myra said.

"How do you know that?"

"Guessing, but the way the dragon is looking down? Just gives that impression." Years of studying valuable objects gave her an instinct for that kind of thing, too. She searched the pile they stood before with a sweeping gaze and didn't see anything immediately that might fit the bill. "We don't have time for a thorough search, do we?"

The longing in her voice was a little embarrassing.

"No. That'll have to do. Let's get out of here." He turned in a slow circle. "How, exactly, do we get out of here?"

The short tunnel they'd moved through to get to the box that had now disappeared was nowhere to be found. Neither was the vertical tunnel they'd climbed down to get this deep underground.

"That's a cloaking spell," she said. "The tunnels are still there. Just invisible."

"Why can't I see through the cloak?" he asked.

"Could you normally?"

"Normally. It's part of dragon physiology, the cloaking, but there are hints that other dragon's pick up."

Interesting. "This isn't a dragon cloak. It's a sort of illusion spell. So maybe that's why you can't see it."

She returned to the area where the box had been and Christopher followed, still frowning at their surroundings. "You do know how to leave, right?"

"I know how to leave," she said.

Escape plans were always part of the plan.

Though sometimes she had to make those plans in the moment and under duress. But she was always looking for the ways to get out.

She stepped close to the area where she'd found the pressure plate to lower the steel box and pressed her foot to the floor in a few places till she found the pressure plate there. This one wasn't bespelled or trapped. It was just there. But if you didn't know what you were looking for, this would be the last level of trap. A thief got in, but then couldn't find a way out.

Only a non-thief would assume that. Which was good for her and Christopher. Jasmin wasn't omnipotent in her security.

The instant she pressed the floor plate, Myra stepped back close to Christopher, tucking her diamond dragon statue into one of her inner vest pockets where it would be safe. Another series of chunking sounds and heavy chains running fast, and then the walls started to come up again, plates unfolding around them, reforming the box room. It was a fun old process to watch, though she did worry about Christopher's head. Fortunately, the box was tall enough for him.

Once it reformed, the opening for the short passage back to the pipe leading up to the ground level opened. It had been there, invisible because of the cloaking spell, but sealed. The box room was necessary to opening that passage to the pipe.

This time, there was no hesitation. From short tunnel to already open antechamber, from antechamber into the narrow pipe, and up the ladder as fast as they could manage to reach the light. If she could have slid up that ladder, she would have.

There was no more dread going in this direction either. In fact, there was almost a push of exhilaration. *Yes! You're going the right way now. Get out. Get out now!*

When she hit the top of the pipe, she scrambled out into the late evening sun, so low now, the forested area was deep in shadows and the sky was starting to turn that shade of purplish orange that came with sunset. The cold air felt like a needed slap in the face after the heat underground.

Or maybe that was just the heat of her anxiety.

Now that they were out, now that she'd done the thing, instead of triumph, all she could think about was Issa and her son in the king's mansion. And Jasmin on the roof facing the king.

Enough time had passed, the entire island of Manhattan might be alight, despite their efforts. A low level of panic started to crawl across her nerves, making her jumpy and jittery.

Christopher emerged from the pipe right behind her, leaping up to the ground from the top ladder rung rather than just crawling out the way Myra had.

Show off.

His wings snapped open instantly, but they still couldn't just fly upward from this position because there were too many trees and tree cover in the way.

"Let me carry you," he said. "We need to move fast."

"You can run fast, too? I thought dragons weren't as fast on the ground as in the air." She jumped into his arms without hesitation, though.

"We're like crocodiles," he said, pausing long enough to meet her gaze. "Slow on the ground is a relative description."

She blinked and he was running. Fast enough she tightened her hold around his neck.

They hit the clearing in a rush, his wings snapped open behind him, and he leapt upward in the space of a heartbeat. They were airborne before Myra's stomach had caught up with the rest of her body.

Laughter would have been inappropriate, but it bubbled in her throat nonetheless because that sort of adrenaline rush was a hit of dopamine to her. But as they climbed, as Christopher blurred their surroundings with his flight speed and cloak, the anxiety returned. There were no signs of smoke or flames on the horizon. Manhattan wasn't on fire. Yet.

But as they raced back to the compound, Myra kept her full attention on the hill where the mansion was. She couldn't see anything clearly at this speed.

Didn't stop her watching anxiously for the red and orange flickering of flames.

FOURTEEN

The mansion was still standing by the time they reached it, circling overhead once before landing on the roof.

Which was now, ominously empty.

There'd been no signs of Jasmin's dragon in the air. And no one on the roof anymore. Which was why Christopher chose to land there instead of returning the way they'd left, through the secret passage that went through the king's hoard. Part of Myra was sort of disappointed about that. She'd wanted to see the hoard again. But most of her was focused on…

"Where is everyone? What's happening?"

Christopher didn't answer—he couldn't know any more than she did, obviously—but his jaw tightened and a muscle there jumped.

They landed lightly, but Christopher didn't put her down immediately and she didn't try to get down immediately. If they had to take flight again quickly, better to be ready to go. The large door that led into the mansion was closed. Christopher didn't move closer to it, just waited.

A heartbeat that felt like an eternity, and the door *kachinked* and then slid upward. Myra's pulse pounded so hard she could hear it, knew Christopher would hear it too. They watched as that door got high enough legs were visible beneath. Beautiful legs in high heels.

Not the dragon king's legs.

Myra swallowed. She was about to pat Christopher's shoulder, encourage him to take off again. Except…

His father. His brother. Issa and her son and her son's father. They were all in there. Somewhere.

When the door fully opened, Jasmin stood in the center of the wide entrance, in human form, her mouth turned down.

And behind her, the dragon king flanked by his son and a handful of his guard.

Myra felt such a shudder of relief she was glad she wasn't standing. Her knees would have given out and that would have been embarrassing.

Jasmin walked toward them, her gaze intent,

but she didn't shift and she didn't hurry. The king followed, at a slower pace, Christopher's brother at his side. The remaining guards waited inside the tunnel.

When she was within fifty yards, Jasmin said, "Did you do it?"

Myra flicked a glance at the king. He lifted his chin in a brief nod. She felt Christopher's arms tighten around her back and legs before he set her slowly onto her feet. He remained at her back and she could practically feel his coiled muscles, ready to move.

Myra didn't approach Jasmin. She reached, slowly, into her pocket and without a word, pulled out the diamond dragon. Held it up for Jasmin to see. It caught the dying sunlight, winking and sparkling like fire.

Appropriate.

The silence that followed felt like it should have caused birds to take flight and animals to scurry into holds. The kind of silence that came with shadows of dread. That sort of silence that meant the hawk was passing overhead.

Myra didn't pull the dragon back but she didn't try to hand it to Jasmin either. She stood with her hand extended, watching Jasmin watch the light dancing in the miniature statue.

When Jasmin looked up and met Myra's gaze, her eyes were black. Solid, impenetrable black.

"You did it."

Myra held perfectly still, unsure what to do now. Christopher moved close enough to her back she could feel his body brushing against hers. There was some comfort in his heat, in the wall of muscle and safety he represented.

Some comfort.

Jasmin glanced back at the king.

The king shrugged, a sort of *I told you so* gesture.

Jasmin's jaw tightened, her full lips pursed. She looked back at Myra. "You win."

Win? Win…what, exactly?

"Keep it," Jasmin said, nodding to the diamond dragon. "It doesn't work without the other part."

Wait, what? Work? What was she talking about?

Myra frowned, but before she could so much as open her mouth to ask, and with a suddenness that had her stumbling back into Christopher, Jasmin shifted to her full dragon form.

The female dragon was…just huge. Myra had thought Christopher was big, but Jasmin's dragon was so tall, her shadow covered the hillside. Her scales were a blackish purple, with lines of orange across her stomach. There were spikes along her back, and tipping her long tail. And her wings. Her wings were so wide, they filled Myra's view. Black as a bat's wings, with a shimmering iridescence that reminded Myra of a geode.

She'd barely had time to take in the massive creature, when the dragon launched into the air, smoothly and so gracefully, there wasn't even a buffeting breeze. By the time Myra looked up, the female was gone. Cloaked or flew away just that fast, she wasn't sure.

Didn't matter.

The female dragon was gone.

Myra blinked up at Christopher. His gaze tracked through the sky for a moment longer before he looked down at her.

"What just happened?" she murmured.

"You won the bet I made with her," the king said, pulling both Myra and Christopher's attention back to him.

"Bet?" she asked.

"I learned that from you. Fortunately, this time, it worked."

And the dragon king smiled.

FIFTEEN

They settled in a comfortable room that was half library, half recreation room. Decorated in dark woods and thick patterned carpets over hard wood floors polished to a shine. Half the walls covered in floor to ceiling bookshelves packed with books. The other half of the room contained card tables, a pool table, a couple of dart boards, and even a few old-fashioned arcade games, though Myra wasn't sure how arcade games and comfortable seats to read went together. The lighting was low, the fire was lit, casting a warm glow around the large but cozy room. And the whiskey was plentiful.

Myra didn't drink often. Dulled senses irritated her. Most of the time. But this was one night when a drink and dulled senses seemed preferable.

The king, his other son—who's name she still hadn't gotten—Issa and the father of her son, along with Christopher and Myra sat in soft, cushioned chairs in the library side of the room, near the fire. Issa's son was being entertained by two of his father's friends. This wasn't a conversation for a child.

"I can't believe she accepted a bet," Myra said, taking another sip of her whiskey.

The idea that the king had pulled that off… It felt like a coup. Like he should win an award for thinking of it. The fact that he gave her credit for the idea instead of claiming it was all his own brilliance left her feeling a little edgy, though. She didn't trust him, or his motivation for crediting her. Felt like a trap of its own.

She was just too tired to sort that part out.

"Jasmin didn't believe any human could possibly manage it," the king said with a shrug. "She didn't believe me when I said you'd broken into my hoard. And she was smug when I bet her that you would breach hers." He shrugged and swirled the whiskey in his cut-crystal glass. "Her arrogance has always been her weakness."

"She's really going to leave me alone?" Issa asked. "Our son?"

"She really is," the king assured. "There's nothing to be done about either of your former bosses I'm afraid. If she didn't kill Dr. Camden before giving chase earlier, she will go kill him now. Dr. Butler was already dead when Jasmin's people picked you up."

The story made Myra's head spin. Or maybe that was the whiskey.

Jasmin had partnered with Dr. Butler to test the waters of a larger insurance fraud scheme she had in mind. It was a game for Jasmin, making money at the expense of other humans. And this particular scheme apparently appealed to her. The plastic surgeons practice was her testing ground to ensure things worked.

When Issa blew the whistle on the scam, Jasmin blamed the two partners for not sufficiently covering their tracks. She'd killed Dr. Butler over it already. She'd kidnapped Issa for information, so the same mistakes weren't made the next time she attempted the scheme. Then she'd intended on killing Issa and the other partner in the business, the man Myra had been thinking of as sportscar man but whose name was Dr. Harry Camden.

Probably they should have tried to save Dr. Camden's life. But by the time Myra learned that his life was in danger, it would have been too late.

And anyway, he'd endangered Issa and her son over greed. Myra wasn't particularly sorry he was no longer a threat.

Myra understood greed. She embraced her own. She was a thief after all. But she drew the line at her avarice destroying other people's lives. It's why she stole from the already obscenely wealthy. She didn't take some poor working mom's last dollar. She stole valuables from the people who wouldn't miss them and from corporations that hoarded wealth. She picked her marks very carefully.

Which was why she only worked for herself. Or had until the dragons came into her life.

She glanced at Christopher, the one dragon she wanted in her life. He sat next to her in a large, low backed chair, slouched in the seat, his long legs stretched out in front of him and crossed at the ankles. He looked relaxed enough outwardly, but she saw the tension in his fingers as he cupped his own whiskey glass in one hand, tapping it gently on the chair's armrest. His gaze was turned down, focused on the slight bounce of liquid in his glass, not looking at the others. He didn't look happy. But no one in the room looked happy, even though they'd technically won the night.

Jasmin had gone. Everyone—or most everyone—was safe. Manhattan hadn't been burned to the ground by an angry female dragon. And Myra had, yet again, pulled off a heist no one thought she could do.

And she got a pretty, sparkling diamond dragon statue out of the mix.

She would love to know what Jasmin had meant by "it doesn't work without the other part" but she intended on researching that when she got home.

The somber mood was probably just shock, she realized. Everyone a little shellshocked from having to deal with a female dragon. Even the king didn't look nearly as smug as he should have after besting Jasmin.

Issa blinked hard at her mostly untouched whiskey and then looked up at her son's father. No one had introduced him yet either. The dragons weren't very good at introductions.

"We should go check on Matias," she said.

The father nodded and offered her his hand as he stood. Myra hid a smile in her drink. Nice to see two parents who weren't together anymore get along like that. And who knew…

She was sometimes a hopeless romantic. She glanced at Christopher again. Her heart did a little dance in her chest, making her feel giddy.

Yeah. She was definitely hopeless.

He caught her gaze, his brooding expression

softening. "If you're ready, I can take you home now, too." He glanced at his brother. "Just need a few minutes."

"Take your time. Didn't have any appointments tonight."

By which she meant, she was still in the planning process for her next theft. Although, after today's dragon hoard raid, her original heist seemed so much less challenging as to be pointless now.

Christopher stood slowly and his brother followed suit, walking ahead of Christopher out of the room. Chistopher stopped beside her before following his brother, setting a hand on her shoulder and giving her a gentle smile.

"Last job for my father," he said. "I promise."

The king snorted but didn't otherwise comment. Christopher and Myra ignored him.

She was too caught up in the expression in Christopher's gaze, that hint of something warm and promising. And suddenly she was smelling sugar cookies again.

She followed him with her gaze as he left, and mostly to herself, she murmured. "Sugar cookies…"

Issa's quiet chuckle drew her attention.

"What is the sugar cookie thing?" she asked Issa.

Issa glanced at her son's father. They both grinned. The father asked, "Do you like sugar cookies?"

"Love them. They're the best cookie. Why?"

"He'll tell you when he's ready," the father said.

"What the hell is your name?" Myra asked suddenly, tired of not knowing and too confused to be polite.

"Havier," he said. "And thank you for helping Issa. I'm not sure we can ever repay you."

She waved that away. "I already got paid." She patted the pocket with the diamond dragon in it. "You're fine."

Issa's grin widened. "You fit in well with them."

She stood with Havier and left before Myra could determine if what Issa had said was a compliment or an insult.

With Havier and Issa's exit, that left Myra alone in the library with the dragon king.

She'd only been alone with the king that one time when he'd walked her through his mansion to a meeting with a wizard. And then, they'd been in public corridors where they passed staff and other dragons regularly on their way to that ill-fated meeting.

"A bet, huh?" she said. "Pretty clever."

"I have my moments." He swirled his whiskey again. The liquid was lower than it had been when his older son had handed him the drink, but she couldn't recall seeing the king take any sips of the alcohol.

"I'm not working for you anymore," she said, bluntly. Because they were alone, she felt like she could be more blunt than she might be allowed in front of witnesses. "I can't. People are already starting to think of me as *your* thief. That can't happen."

The king's eyes narrowed, his only change in expression.

In the firelight, his changeable eyes were more green than blue. And there seemed to be more silver in his dark hair than there'd been the last time she'd seen him, but she still wasn't sure if he'd been adding silver dye to his hair or not, so she wasn't sure if this was just to deepen the effect of him looking older and distinguished or not.

"Our association could be very profitable for you," the king said. "Already has been." He nodded to the pocket where she'd tucked her new acquisition.

"The jobs you talk me into have gone consistently pear-shaped, been lies, or put me in the way of people who try to kill me. I can do profitable on my own, without that added hassle."

One sardonic brow rose, but then his expression turned brooding, a frown turning down his mouth.

The look had her nerves tightening. She'd had more than enough of dancing around volatile dragon shifters tonight. She didn't *want* to be on the king's bad side. But she needed to put an end to him thinking she'd work for him anymore. Here and now.

When he met her gaze, his expression made her stomach tight. She couldn't explain why. He looked angry maybe. Or resentful. Definitely broody and annoyed.

"You'll continue to see Christopher?" he asked.

The comment felt like a change in subject, but she went with the flow. "I will. If he wants to keep seeing me."

Not that they'd reached the stage of anything…official. But after everything they'd been through, she knew she wanted something more, wanted all those promises that buzzed between them and she'd been putting off exploring. She trusted Christopher. In a way she trusted very few people. Maybe no one else since her parents. All on its own, that was an experience she wanted to explore more.

And if that involved getting the huge, hunky,

sexy Christopher naked finally, she'd be open to that, too.

The king growled at her, the growl containing that quiet hiss that was such a dragon sound. The hairs on the back of her neck prickled.

But she didn't back down. She wasn't going to be scared off from seeing Christopher. And she wasn't going to work for the king anymore. And he was just going to have to get used to both ideas.

She did grip her glass a little tighter, and she grew very aware of the distance between her seat and the closed library door.

The king stood abruptly, so fast, Myra scrambled to her feet, too. Not even sure what she meant to do. Run away? Her instincts thought that might be a good idea. Her logic knew the effort would be futile. The king was a shifter. He moved a lot faster than she did.

The library door opened at just that moment, Christopher standing in the doorway.

The king snarled at her and then at his son. "Fine," he spit out. "But only because *he* smells like sugar cookies."

The king stalked out, his half-full glass of whiskey perched precariously on the armrest of the chair he'd abandoned so abruptly. Christopher stepped aside to let him leave, then turned back toward her, frowning.

Myra was left with her mouth hanging open. She shook her head at Christopher's raised brows. "I don't know how to explain," she answered his unspoken question.

Christopher came fully into the room, walking toward her slowly, giving her time to admire him. She loved watching him move. There was a subtle grace and strength. Sexy as sin.

"So," he said, when he stood close enough she had to crane her neck up to meet his gaze.

"So." She smiled. "Interesting day."

"Wrong kind of interesting."

She chuckled. "Everything okay with your brother?"

"Fine. I think." He shook his head. "It's nothing."

Sure. Nothing. But if he wasn't prepared to talk about it, she'd give him his privacy. Her curiosity did not give her a right to all his secrets. Even if she wouldn't mind knowing a few.

She did ask, "What the hell is his name? You all suck at introductions."

Christopher's mouth quirked. "We...offer our names to each other when we're ready to allow another dragon to know it. There are formal aspects of dragon naming and exchanging dragon names. That social instinct means we sometimes forget to offer our names to the humans we interact with."

"Oh. Shit, have I been breaking dragon protocol or something by asking everyone for their names?" She just realized she'd demanded the names of a bunch of dragons in passing because she got tired of not knowing what to call them. That included Christopher. She hadn't realized she was doing something the dragons considered rude.

But Christopher said, "It's not a custom that applies to humans. You haven't done anything wrong. We just forget to introduce ourselves, that's all."

"Okay. But since it is a custom, you don't have to tell me your brother's name. It's fine."

"Like I said, the custom doesn't apply to humans. His name is Thomas."

"Not Tom."

"Not. Tom."

Her lips twitched. There really was a dragon thing about names. None of them wanted their names shortened and got very growly about it all. "Thomas. Will he be offended if I call him by name since he never introduced himself?"

"No. He'll assume I told you. Or the king."

"The king gives me no names." He hadn't

even called Christopher by name when sending her to rescue him.

"What did the two of you talk about?"

"How I wouldn't work for him anymore."

"And he said?"

"I think that last barked 'fine' before he stomped out was in reference to that. But also it could have been in reference to me telling him I would continue seeing you." Her gaze danced away from his as a strange bout of shyness swept up her cheeks, heat she was afraid was a blush. "If you want to, of course."

Christopher lifted her chin, gently easing her face up so she had to look him in the eye. "Of course I want," he said quietly. "I thought you realized that."

"I suppose I do. Obvious, isn't it? But… A lot's happened. I don't want to assume anything."

"I was worried, after you saw my dragon, you wouldn't want… anymore."

"Your dragon is beautiful. Terrifying of course, but that's dragons for you." She tried to force a smile. Tried to lighten the moment. The seriousness of it all made her antsy even as she wanted Christhoper to be serious about her. Because she was quite serious about him.

"You're nervous, though," he said.

"Not of your dragon."

Of what this meant between them? Yes. Especially knowing his father did not approve. If Christopher was just anyone, she wouldn't care about parental approval. As it was, she didn't care enough to back off from whatever this was with her and Christopher. But him being the son of the dragon king, and the dragon king not liking their more personal relationship, was a complication.

A complication they'd one day have to confront.

But maybe not tonight. Maybe not all at once.

"You want to go for a night flight?" she asked, leaning into him so their bodies were pressed together. His arms came up around her automatically, as if that was just naturally the thing they did. She loved that.

"Haven't had enough flying for one day?" His soft, sexy smile melted her. In a good way.

"Never," she said. "Not with you."

That was as close as she'd gotten to some kind of declaration. But it was enough for now. And obviously enough for him, because his sexy smile deepened and he pulled her closer and lowered his head to her. She rose on her toes to meet him. His lips were soft. His hold firm. And that melty feeling that had started moments earlier got infinitely more melty.

She sank into the kiss, opening to him, letting

the play of her tongue against his and the grip of her fingers on his shoulders show him what was difficult for her to say. Heat washed through her, a good kind of heat that made her comfortable and restless at the same time. Left her breathless. And needy.

And happy.

By the time they pulled out of the kiss, Myra was breathing hard and had forgotten where they were. Not hard to do when Christopher had his mouth on hers.

"Let's fly," he said.

She grinned, nodded, and took his hand when he led her from the library.

"You ever going to tell me about the sugar cookie thing?" she asked, bumping his arm and giving him a sideways look.

He also looked down at her from the corner of his eyes. "You haven't figured it out yet?"

She scowled. "Should I have?"

His rumbling chuckle had her skin tingling, reminding her of the feel of his lips on hers, the way he tasted, the way his warm, hard body felt pressed against hers. He glanced down at her again, his brows raised slightly, his smile sexy enough to make her stumble a step.

"I'll explain it," he said, as he led her outside onto the roof.

The cold night air cooled some of the heat in her cheeks and body but not enough. She still felt weak-kneed and restless and she needed to be in his arms. Needed to be soaring over the city with his wings above them, her arms wrapped around his neck.

She jumped up into his waiting arms, which put her face close to his. "You will?"

"Eventually." He hugged her tighter to his body as his wings snapped out behind him, the rush of scales over his shoulders under her hands a soft tickle.

Okay. More dragon shifter stuff she'd have to wait to learn. "When you're ready," she said more than asked.

He glanced toward the sky, then met her gaze. "When you are."

And he launched into the air, leaving Myra's stomach far below. And her heart firmly lodged in her throat.

THANK YOU

Thanks for reading The Femme Fatale Job! I hope you enjoyed spending more time with Myra and Christopher. As well as this first introduction to one of the rare and terrifying female dragon shifters! We will see them again. And that other part of the statue Myra found... Well, let's just say that will likely pop up at some point in the future, too. But not in the next episode. This is a series I intend to write many more books in because there are lots of stories still to tell, and I'm having a whole lot of fun with them. I hope you'll join me on that journey.

Also, have you guessed what the sugar cookie smell is all about? *grin*

For more on my paranormal romance and urban fantasy books—as well as everything I write—check out my store, KatSimonsBooks, or visit my website. If you'd like to get all the news direct to your inbox, consider joining my monthly newsletter. New subscribers get two exclusive shorts—one from my Cary Redmond urban fantasy series, and one from my Tiger Shifters paranormal romance series (as you might have noticed, I like shifter stories.) You'll also get cover reveals, occasional excerpts, sales alerts, discounts to the store, and much more.

If you'd prefer, you can always follow my author page at BookBub, on Facebook, or at any of your favorite retail vendors. You can also find me on Instagram where I tend to talk about baking and sporting events and travel, but also post about my books sometimes too.

Thanks again for reading this latest adventure in the Dragon Thief series!

~Kat

Don't miss the next story in the
Dragon Thief series!

THE SCAVENGER JOB

Keep reading for an excerpt!

THE SCAVENGER JOB

EXCERPT

ONE

Myra clung to Christopher's shoulders, her arms wrapped tightly around his neck as they soared over the city, his wings spread out above them, the nighttime New York City skyline below. The last day had been strange and complicated. And she was still deciding how she felt about it all.

Not that the last couple of months hadn't all been complicated and strange. Breaking into the dragon king's hoard had thrown her into a world she had never planned on visiting, nonetheless staying. And yet now, here she was. Happy to be in Christopher's arms. Happy they'd survived the last few days.

But leery of the world she now seemed to be

part of because she wanted to stay in Christopher's arms.

The night air bit sharply at her cheeks. Winter in full swing now. But the cold felt good. And Christopher's body temperature was so warm, she was comfortable in his arms during the flight.

A flight that had been her idea. They'd been dancing around their feelings for each other for the last few months. Or rather, she'd been dancing. In and out. Not sure if she really wanted to let more happen between them because it would mean staying at the edge of the dragon shifter world. Also not prepared to stop seeing him. Since they'd first met, she'd been attracted to him. Now, what she felt was…more. Enough she was willing to try something she never did.

They banked over Midtown, angling toward the west side of the island and his apartment at the top of one of the many high-rises in the area. Not the tallest building, but tall enough that his large open patio on the top floor gave him plenty of room to fly in and land. No need for elevators when you could do a partial shift and have wings.

As his feet settled onto the stone balcony, he tightened his grip on her, as if he didn't want to set her down. She didn't mind. She wasn't in a hurry to get out of his arms either.

"You're sure about this?" he asked.

Myra nodded. "Never been more sure of anything."

And after the last day, she meant those words with her whole being.

THE WATERS OF THE UPPER BAY FLOWED PAST AS Myra leaned over the edge of the ferry rail, enjoying the cut of the cold air and the whip of wind. When she looked up, the grand lady herself, the Statue of Liberty, stood glimmering in the sunlight across the water. Despite living in New York her entire life, she'd never been out to the statue. Maybe one day.

Now, she had other plans.

Which started in, of all places, Staten Island.

She loved riding on the Staten Island ferry, but she rarely got off and went into Staten Island. She hung out in St. George station, maybe got an ice cream, and then got back onto the next ferry returning to Manhattan. Mostly, she did this for the free boat ride. She could afford other options, she supposed. But when she was a kid, this free trip was what they could afford, and it had been one of her favorite things to do with her parents.

Still one of her favorite things to do.

"You're going to fall into the water." A deep

voice behind her. "And if you do, I'm not rescuing you."

She could hear both his worry and his hesitance. "Of course you will." She chuckled. "You couldn't resist rescuing me if you tried."

She smiled as she turned to face him. At nearly seven foot tall, Christopher's head came perilously close to the top of the roof on this lower deck. He sort of hunched to accommodate the occasional crossbeam, but it didn't help hide his size.

Nothing could really hide him when he was out among humans. Even without pictures of him out in public, she'd heard the others on the ferry whispering that he must be one of the dragon shifters. Which, he was. But fortunately, no one realized he was one of the dragon king's sons. There were no pictures of the royal family allowed in public. She hadn't understood why when the king had first informed her of the dictate. Now, after spending more time with Christopher, she realized it was a blessing for his sons, to have some semblance of privacy in a world that was *intensely* curious about them.

He really wasn't the kind of man who blended into the background, though. Dark messy hair, deep blue eyes, wide shoulders. There was a lot of potential for classical handsomeness to him, and yet he wasn't. The angles of his face were too sharp and the assembly of those features could have been described as awkward. No, not classically handsome. But compelling. Hard not to notice. Impossible not to look at twice.

She liked to think of his face as interesting. She was certainly interested in that face. Interested in the rest of him, too. And that interest had moved past simple lust now. Way past. Which was one of the many reasons for this trip to Staten Island. Even if he didn't realize it yet.

"I will absolutely let you fall into the river if you keep leaning so far over the rail," he said, hands on his hips.

She laughed. "First of all, we both know you wouldn't." He had a thing about damsels in distress. Couldn't let them remain in distress. Had to help. Some of the other dragons considered it a character flaw. She loved it about him. "Secondly, I can swim."

"Why am I not surprised."

"You're not? Damn, I'm becoming predictable."

"Never." His expression softened into a smile that made her stomach dance. She loved that smile. "Are you going to tell me what we're doing now?"

"Nope. It's a surprise."

"I'm not crazy about surprises."

"I know. But you'll love this one. I promise."

"Are we stealing anything?"

"Nothing that will be missed."

"That doesn't instill much confidence."

She winked. "You want some hot chocolate? It's a ferry tradition for me in the winter."

She was bundled up in a long wool coat, gloves, scarf, and thick wooly cap. Beneath she wore her work clothes. Black yoga pants, black shirt, her trusty, multi-pocket vest. But the coat, scarf, and hat were all bright. White coat. Red hat and scarf. Green gloves. She was a beacon of winter colors.

The expression on Christopher's face when they'd met at the ferry station, and she'd shown up wearing something that wasn't black, had been a delight to witness. The shock. And then the slow sweep of his gaze that had set those now familiar tingles dancing in her stomach. She had her hair down—which was rare—and had gone to the effort of wearing makeup. She even had mid-height, chunky-heeled boots on. The heels did nothing to get her anywhere near his height. He still had at least a foot and a half on her. But the heels made her calves look good in her tight leggings.

It was fun surprising him. She managed it occasionally. And she enjoyed it every time.

He was dressed for show, too. She appreciated that he'd even worn shoes so he didn't stand out too much. He hated wearing shoes for too long. His black wool winter coat and a scarf he sort of threw around his neck gave a nod to the winter. He needed neither. He could control his body temperature—most of the time—and didn't feel the cold the way a human might. When you flew and spent a lot of time at altitude with nothing but a few scales between you and the biting air, you needed to be able to stay warm.

He looked her over as another icy breeze blew across the open side of the bottom deck. There were only a few hearty souls out here. Most remained in the relative protection of the inside cabins.

"Hot chocolate would be good if it means getting you off that railing."

"I am not *on* the railing," she said, bumping her shoulder against his arm as she led him back inside. "If I were *on* the railing, I'd be closer to your height."

And she was not trying to draw that kind of attention on this trip.

With only a couple of days left till Christmas,

there were a lot more tourists on the ferry than usual for a winter afternoon on a weekend. If there was no compelling reason to take the ferry in the winter—like going to and from work—a lot of locals gave it a pass. But the ferry was, nonetheless, packed with people. Crowds inside making the lines at the snack stands surprisingly long. There were a few decorations up around the stand, some red and green tinsel, a menorah in honor of Hanukah, some fairy lights winking in white around the order window.

Myra loved this time of year. She liked the cold. But she also loved all the lights and twinkling colors. Not unlike actual treasure. Which she also loved.

The hot chocolate was delicious, though so hot she burned her tongue with her first sip.

"Can't take the heat?" Christopher asked, with a sexy smile.

"I can take heat just fine," she said, trying not to fall into his gaze and failing miserably.

"Need any help with the burn?" His gaze dropped to her mouth. "I could kiss it better."

Yeah he could.

A little purple light played over his irises, and his pupils were narrowed from the bright sunlight spilling in through all the windows lining the cabin. They'd taken a seat near a window that looked out toward the bridges. She loved the view of Lady Liberty, but watching the Brooklyn, Manhattan, and in the distance, the Williamsburg bridges was pretty stunning too. Definitely in New York with that view. But in that moment, all of her attention was captured by Christopher. And that faint purple light in his eyes.

Her stomach tumbled with now-familiar giddiness. Very soon they were going to have to do something about all this tension between them. And for her, very soon was sooner now than it had been a few months ago.

"We'd better wait on that kissing," she murmured. She was a little afraid if they started, she'd embarrass herself by forgetting they were in public.

That "forgetting herself" part had become increasingly more likely. And her resistance to forgetting herself increasingly thinner as the weeks rolled past. Everything about Christopher hit her lusty buttons and left her swoony. From his inability to resist a damsel in distress to his impressive height to the way he accepted her just as she was without trying to force her into a more conventional box.

Things with his father might be easier if she were a more ordinary human. Her being a thief, and a magical one at that, meant she was useful to the dragon king, but not his first choice for his son's romantic interests. Christopher didn't seem to care. And his father seemed to have given up any thought of interfering. At least, he'd made a show of giving up. Whether he had or not was anyone's guess. It was impossible to tell with the dragon king.

But the king had stopped attempting to hire her. Finally. Stopped trying to make her one of "his" people. Stopped trying to control her.

And that had made all the difference.

Now she just needed to do this one thing. One thing before "forgetting herself" completely.

Don't miss the final story in SEASON ONE
of the Dragon Thief series!

THE SCAVENGER JOB

Out now!

Join Kat's Newsletter

Stay Up-to-Date

On all Kat's News, Updates, and fun extras

New Subscriber Get Two Exclusive Stories Just for Signing up!

bit.ly/KatSimonsNewsletter

The CARY REDMOND Series

GOT TROUBLE?

Don't Miss a Single Book in this
Action-Packed Romantic Urban Fantasy Series

Books By Kat Simons

Dragon Thief Series

SEASON ONE

Dragon Thief

The Chicago Job

The Poisons Book Job

The Vault Job

The Femme Fatale Job

The Scavenger Job

SEASON TWO

The Crown of Kingship Job

The Green Scroll Job

The Payback Job

Pick Your Genre Collections

Who Steals a Dragon

The Cary Redmond Series

* The Trouble Black Cats and Demons * The Trouble
with Ghouls and Serial Killers * The Trouble with

Leopard Queens and Shifter Wars * The Trouble with Baby Gods and Vampires * The Trouble with Magic and Faery Curses * The Trouble with Wizards and Old Enemies * The Trouble with Death and Demon Gods

The Cary Redmond Series Box Set Books 1-3

Cary Redmond Short Stories

* When Cary Met Jaxer * When Cary Met Pickles * When Cary Met Marianne * When Cary Met Lucy * When Cary Met Angie * Cary and Deacon (Try to) Go on a Date * Date Night Take Two * Third Date's the Charm * Cary vs the Goblin King * Dinner with the Joneses * Cary and the Cursed Jack-O'-Lantern * Cary and the Demon Witch * Cary Goes to Hawaii * Cary Holidays * Cary and Dragons and Goblins * Cary's Galentine's Day * Cary at the Haunt and Howl * Cary's Leprechaun Troubles * Cary's Beltane Night Out *

When Cary Met the Good Guys (Collection 1)

Dates, Dinners, and Other Disasters (Collection 2)

Witches and Weavers and Ghosts, Oh Boy (Collection 3)

A Very Cary Holiday (Collection 4)

Romancing the Leopard: A Tiger Shifters-Cary Redmond Crossover Novel

Tiger Shifters Series

* Once Upon a Tiger * Along Came a Tiger * Here There Be Tigers * Her Tiger To Take * To Tempt a Tiger * Down Will Come Tiger * To Catch a Tiger * What a Tiger Wants * Taming Her Tiger

Tiger Shifters Series Vol 1 (Books 1 - 3)

Tiger Shifters Series Vol 2 (Books 4 - 6)

Seven Families Series

Wolf Family

Darkness in Stone

Redemption in Stone

Fated in Stone

Wolf in Stone: A Seven Families Box Set, Books 1-3

Demon Witch Series

Howling Dreadful

Moonlit Strange

Bone Lantern Witch

Spiderweb Witch

Storm Shadow Witch

Darkling Mist Witch

Joan of Kerry Series

Joan of Kerry: Joan and the Abhartach

Joan and the Leprechaun

Joan and the Kraken

Joan and the Selkie

Joan and the Goblins

Haunts and Howls Collections

Haunts and Howls and Guardian Spells

Haunts and Howls Where Demons Dwell

Haunts and Howls and Jesters Bells

Haunts and Howls and Fairy Dales

*Tombstone Wizard * The Unshattered Sword *
Destiny Through the Cats Eyes * Going Out of
Business: Everything's for Sale * Anger Management *
Demonic Dates * Friday's Curious Shop * The Museum
of Small Art's Everyman * Burning Inside a Stone
Circle * Bored Questless * I Just Ate a Bug * Ting Ling
* Sophie Saves the World * Black Water Hawthorns
*To Dance in Fallow Fields at Midnight *

More Books by Kat Simons

Contemporary Romances

Designed for You

Poinsettias and Possibilities

Mystery and Thrillers

Ross and O'Neill Adventures

Galileo's Pendulum

Percy James Mysteries

Movies May Murder

Cookies Can't Crime

Diamonds Do Damage

Replicas Risk Ruin

Vacation Deadly: An Action Adventure Thriller
Collection

About the Author

Kat Simons earned her Ph.D. in animal behavior, working with animals as diverse as dolphins and deer. She brought her experience and knowledge of biology to her paranormal romance and urban fantasy fiction, where she delights in taking nature and turning it on its ear. She writes urban fantasy, contemporary fantasy, and paranormal romance in series which combine action adventure, the otherworldly, and a frequent dose of sexy romance.

The newest book in her bestselling romantic urban fantasy series about Protector Cary Redmond, The Trouble with Shifters and Fae Courts, sees a new direction for the intrepid Protector, her sexy leopard shifter mate, and the entire crew. Kat also launched a new novella length Paranormal Romance series that follows the adventures of a magical thief and the dragon shifter prince she just can't seem to shake—and really doesn't want to. The first season of the Dragon Thief series released throughout 2024.

Season Two begins in 2025 with The Crown of Kingship Job.

For something a little different, Kat also publishes fantasy, science fiction, and the occasional hockey romance under the name Isabo Kelly (https://www.isabokelly.com).

After traveling the world, living in places like Hawaii, Germany, and Ireland, Kat now lives in New York City with her family and a library's worth of books.

For more on Kat and her future books

Website: https://www.katsimons.com/
Newsletter: https://bit.ly/KatSimonsNewsletter

KatSimonsBooks

https://www.katsimonsbooks.com
https://www.TheCafeatKatSimonsBooks.com

Social Media

Facebook Page: https://www.facebook.com/
KatSimonsAuthor
BookBub: https://www.bookbub.com/authors/kat-
simons
Bluesky: https://bsky.app/profile/katsimons.bsky.
social
Instagram: https://www.instagram.com/isabokelly/
Threads: https://www.threads.net/@isabokelly